THE MEGABUILDERS OF
Queenston Park

Published by Wild River Books
P.O. Box 53
Stockton, New Jersey 08559
www.wildriverconsultingandpublishing.com

Distributed by Wild River Consulting & Publishing, LLC.

Design and composition by:
Tim Ogline / Ogline Design for Wild River Consulting & Publishing, LLC.

Publisher's Cataloging-In-Publication Data
Keeley, Edmund Leroy
  The Megabuilders of Queenston Park/Edmund Leroy Keeley—1st ed.
ISBN: 978-0-9839188-4-4

1. Literature. 2. Fiction. 3. Princeton. 4. Ecology. 5. Edmund Leroy Keeley

The Megabuilders of Queenston Park was partially funded by a grant from the Princeton University Committee on Research in the Humanities and Social Sciences.

Wild River Books's mission has been generously funded by alumni of Princeton University.

Printed in the United States of America

First Edition

THE MEGABUILDERS OF
Queenston Park

A NOVEL

BY EDMUND KEELEY

WILD RIVER BOOKS

FICTION

The Libation
The Gold-Hatted Lover
The Impostor
Voyage to a Dark Island
A Wilderness Called Peace
School for Pagan Lovers
Some Wine for Remembrance

NON-FICTION

Modern Greek Writers (ed. with Peter Bien)
Cavafy's Alexandria
Modern Greek Poetry: Voice and Myth
R. P. Blackmur: Essays, Memoirs, Texts (ed.with Edward Cone and Joseph Frank)
The Salonika Bay Murder: Cold War Politics and the Polk Affair
Albanian Journal: The Road To Elbasan
George Seferis and Edmund Keeley: Correspondence, 1951-1971
Inventing Paradise: The Greek Journey, 1937-1947
On Translation: Reflections and Conversations
Borderlines: A Memoir

POETRY IN TRANSLATION

Six Poets of Modern Greece (with Philip Sherrard)
George Seferis: Collected Poems (with Philip Sherrard
C. P. Cavafy: Passions and Ancient Days (with George Savidis)
C. P. Cavafy: Selected Poems (with Philip Sherrard)
Odysseus Elytis: The Axion Esti (with George Savidis)
C. P. Cavafy: Collected Poems (with Philip Sherrard and George Savidis)
Angelos Sikelianos: Selected Poems (with Philip Sherrard)
Ritsos in Parentheses
Voices of Modern Greece: A Greek Quintet (with Philip Sherrard)
Odysseus Elytis: Selected Poems (with Philip Sherrard)
Yannis Ritsos: Exile and Return, Selected Poems 1968-74
Yannis Ritsos: Repetitions, Testimonies, Parentheses
The Essential Cavafy
A Century Of Greek Poetry
(ed. with Peter Bien, Peter Constantine, and Karen Van Dyck)
The Greek Poets: Homer to the Present
(ed. with Peter Constantine, Rachel Hadas, and Karen Van Dyck)
Yannis Ritsos: Diaries of Exile (with Karen Emmerich)

FICTION IN TRANSLATION

Vassilis Vassilikos: The Plant, The Well, The Angel (with Mary Keeley)

For Joy E. Stocke and Karen Kennerly
πιστές σύντροφοι

CHAPTER

Cassie remembered being amused by the visiting writer from Texas who'd called Princeton New Jersey a sleepy town some twenty years ago in a *Town Topics* interview. Maybe fairly sleepy back then, but now sometimes not sleepy enough from one point of view, all growth, all expansion, all development building here and there or single mansions larger and larger. Anyway, how much could a visitor from Texas really know about Princeton, New Jersey? Maybe even back then Texas was so full of fast-moving people that a mostly quiet and green piece of the Garden State could seem, well, languid to a writer who wrote musicals about bordellos in southern borderland towns.

Of course she herself really knew nothing about Texas, except that Nick liked to call it Bushland and sometimes make fun of it. But when it came to sleepy towns, she knew a few things a Texan wasn't likely to know, beginning with her own home town: narrow lanes and small blue windows hiding anything that moved behind their whitewashed walls, a beautiful domestic prison on the Aegean Sea that didn't let you

travel very far unless you were lucky. That first one not as colorless but
certainly less free than the spreading white city of cement prisons to the
south that she'd moved to during her early university days, and certainly
closed-in compared to almost any town she'd later visited in Italy. But
none of these anything like the tree-rich broad-lawned Princeton she'd
finally migrated to, even if that fast-talking redheaded exiled Russian
poet opened his local reading back then by thanking his friends in
Prison, New Jersey, for the invitation. Maybe that was meant to be a
joke, or maybe he really had some trouble speaking the language in those
days—anyway, who was she with her accent to be casting stones?

OK, so the town was a bit sleepy to outsiders, but it didn't make you
feel confined, crowded, always watched by your neighbors not in the
older section to the south with the grand houses and spreading lawns,
or the middle section with the tall university buildings and their landscaping, not even those parts of the oldest section now under renovation
that Nick said used to be for the sons of slaves brought north to serve
the student sons of southern landowners in the nineteenth century. My
God. Slaves as recently as that, how could it be so in America?

And in her section of Queenston Park, the houses might be small by
comparison to others in Princeton, mostly ranch style and split-levels,
but the lots were big. Some really big like hers and Nick's, so that you
had the sense of space and open air and things growing, all the way from
the ground up to the giant trees left over from the farm land it used to
be. Yes, it was good, this sense of space, but how long would it be there?
Not long, unless people in her portion of the Township began to wake
up to what was happening.

At least a few in her reading group were talking about it, as alarmed
as she was about builders moving in to take over any land they could buy
with houses they could easily tear down and replace with huge houses
towering above their neighbors and adding to the still uncontrolled

flooding problems, some of them ugly houses made out of pre-fabricated sections, rectangular boxes piled up on top of each other and nailed together, with no connection to what was already in the neighborhood. Three new mansions already going up in Queenston Park, all with five or six bedrooms, some with five or six baths, three garages, roofs that seemed as tall as most trees. And the houses that once belonged to those lots, sometimes still lived in by the first owner going back to the Second World War, small but still solid enough, gone now, vanished, knocked down and hauled away as though trash for disposal who knows where. How could anybody let that happen to a house they'd lived in that long? Maybe a time came when they simply couldn't help it for one reason or another, God forbid. Some of them, but surely not all. Maybe houses meant too much to her, so she just didn't see things the way others did. Or maybe the neighborhood and the rest of the Township were letting it happen because most people weren't really paying attention, other things on their minds, if not asleep, halfway there.

Time to head home. Nick reckoned he'd walked a good two miles in open country along the canal pathway from Kingston to the Harrison Street bridge and back—well, not exactly open, but there were no houses on one side of the pathway and those across Lake Carnegie, when you could see them through the trees, were far enough away to be no distraction from the spread of green foliage unless you made them so. He'd needed that space to think clearly, to work it all out in his mind before he brought it up with Cassie, find how best to explain in a general way this early retirement plan he'd actually been thinking about how long now?—anyway long enough for it to seem at least rational from his point of view. Of course there was a good chance she would consider it curious at best, maybe nonsensical, maybe even threatening, whether she actually went there straight away or just gave him a look that seemed to see right through him and well beyond.

Cassandra of the green eyes, tolerant to a fault most of the time, her expression more amused than critical when he got his Greek verbs wrong again, and that smile, open-ended, unembarrassed, if the day came in right, her sun in its just place. And still looking young enough to make most people think the ten years that separated them were closer to twenty, not exactly baby-faced but still girlish, hair still dark enough to be startling against her light olive skin, her figure what it was when they first met, the same seductive turn of her head every now and then despite her being a bit old-fashioned in her manners and sometimes in her outlook.

But it was her sun's dark side that had him a bit worried. Her look that could stab you if she thought you mean or foolish, and her tongue suddenly cutting sharp. At least the retirement issue—if that's what it was likely to become—would be strictly between the two of them, their daughter Lydia's welfare and peace of mind no longer involved the way it used to be before she married and moved to California, only their own future affected at this point. Still, he doubted that she'd settle for a skeptical look and silence. Retire at sixty-five before you have to? Isn't that a foolish thing to do? How would you keep busy? How would I keep you out of my hair?

He'd simply have to convince her that he had no intention of actually retiring from serious work, just putting the College and its minor discontents behind him. The point was for him to be entirely free to decide what he wanted to do and then have the time to do it. Not that he could claim the College, even if increasingly ambitious, was really demanding after all these years, certainly not as demanding as Princeton University would have been from the very start had that possibility worked out back then, back when he was admittedly a competitive overachiever like most of the others around him. Oh well, one fate saves you from another, as Cassie would put it. Even with the Classics generally on the rise in the country, student elections in his department at the College were still modest along with much else that was modest, no particular pressure to publish more than he already had, no pressure of any kind really if you taught your classes with sufficient imagination and did your share of administrative work. But the point now was to be free, finally, to give his pride some room.

He could hear his old unforgiving senior thesis advisor mumble from his grave: class of '63 at Princeton and still fiddling away in the backwaters? He thought he'd quieted that voice long ago when he'd swallowed his pride and settled for living in Princeton even if he wasn't teaching there and even if he would have a good half-hour commute through the back roads to the upper edge of the Pine Barrens. Small price, he'd then decided, for giving Cassie's first American days the benefit of what a famous university town had to offer its residents by way of its theatre, the public lectures, whatever. And if the place could sometimes show a stuffy side, an arrogant side, things had begun to change even back then so that it was no longer the quaint ceremonious village of puny demigods on stilts that Einstein had called it in his time. You'd have to call it a city now, still relatively small but expanding in all directions, the University itself expanding —anyway, to hell with ancient voices out of Hades, Cassie's down-to-earth voice all that really concerned him these days.

How to keep busy in retirement? Never mind the big projects he'd left behind and finally lost along the way, translations of Apollonius of Rhodes' grand epic and Callimachus's brilliant epigrams while he dallied his way through lesser poets in the Palatine Anthology. What about shifting to something closer to his heart, following in the footsteps

of the obscure namesake he'd run across in Webster's at one point, Sir
Somebody Mandeville, pseudonym of an unidentified author of travel
books, who might serve as a ghostly inspiration for him to return to
the several books of that genre he'd outlined in his mind over the years?
Travel in the Byways of Europe and the Middle East. Or *The Long Journey:
To Strive, to Seek, to Find*—the title could wait.

The real problem was travel. That had once been easy, in fact
essential. The two of them ending up in Italy from different directions
was what had brought them together, then traveling across Europe to end
up in the Mediterranean had set the pattern for the summer months and
sabbaticals—except for this one, where the thought of settling abroad for
three months had somehow seemed a distraction more than a resource in
his mind and anyway hadn't reached the stage of serious discussion with
Cassie before it had become too late to implement reasonably. It seemed
they'd both become too settled, after more than thirty years both tied
to where they were most comfortable, where they each had their own
space and their own routine of work, he mostly in his study, she mostly
taking care of the house and keeping up with this group or that. And
the neighborhood had become simply their neighborhood after all these
years. So how could you write about travel without traveling? Without
returning to the old places that could rouse your memory and new ones
to save you from relying on nostalgia as your only guide? That would
take more thought. That would—

Now what in God's name is this? He decided to pull over and have
a look before turning into his driveway. He was certain the sign hadn't
been there when he headed out for the lake because he'd noticed the
condition of the patch of front lawn next door where the sign now
stood, that bit clearly in need of attention, really out of tune with all the
rest that old man Truex had created over there as an amateur landscaper
who was still capable of covering the best part of his vast back lawn with

small ponds and miniature bridges and carefully manicured shrubs in some kind of privately conceived pattern that apparently reminded him of his childhood in Belgium. Just what did this sign mean? That the old man had moved on somewhere in or out of our world?

He'd seen people arriving by car over there on and off in recent weeks, and he'd had a conversation several months ago about the old man's heart condition when they'd happened to pick up their mail at the same time, a rare meeting since the man's Swiss wife had died of cancer five years ago, but no talk of that place going up for sale and no particular evidence that the man had moved out. Who is this "Randolph Parker, Builder" of "Solar Estates" anyway? Serving Princeton and Chapel Hill? Strange alliance. Or is it? Another university town, and they say some of the architecture down there was modeled on Princeton's.

Not keeping up with the neighbors was of course his fault and Cassie's as much as anybody's, though one of the attractions of living in Queenston Park all these years was the quiet space, most people tending to keep their distance, as the houses themselves did, generally well spaced so that nobody crowded anybody else, some almost invisible behind the giant trees in the larger lots, everybody left to go about his or her own business, free to make their friends wherever they chose, a few gatherings for group meetings of one kind or another but the neighborhood parties rare, hardly more than a nod of partial recognition among the passing walkers and joggers but still a nod, and sometimes a friendly glance across this or that University activity open to the public. But not to know whether the man next door was dead or alive seemed to be going too far. Even for Princeton.

And now this Solar Estates out of the blue. Ominous. Sounded like one of these developers who'd taken over yet another spread of open country on the outskirts of the town and put up a huge colony of monster houses nudging each other for a bit of elbow room as they were lined up in squares or circles or at calculated odd angles. And always a fancy name that had a bucolic touch or a historical echo and in any case a Princeton address even if halfway to New Brunswick. But fortunately the lot next door was just one lot, an unusually large lot yet meant for a single house only, as the Queenston Park Housing Board would insist whatever the zoning laws elsewhere. No subdividing permitted. No crowding. Size and design subject to approval, etc. So why worry? Surely there were additional Township regulations. And whatever might be going on next door, he and Cassie had their own domain, their own small piece of inviolable America.

Randy Parker eased back against the mailbox to see if the sign Tim had put up rather casually earlier in the week was now finally more level than he'd found it. He was pleased that Tim had gone along with putting Princeton ahead of Chapel Hill even though it was the newer of their two offices by a decade. Who would know the time difference anyway? What counted was the territory ahead, Princeton, NJ, the Athens of America according to what he'd read somewhere, Einstein's territory, rich country any way you looked at it. And from his recent survey of the place, it was ripe for exploitation—at least in the Township area along the back road to New York, where the lots were still large and the houses relatively small, easy teardowns.

As far as he could see, the prospects were grand, the future unlimited, he and Tim just at the start of transforming the region in a way that was profitable for everybody involved—owner, builder, buyer—the whole development enterprise truly democratic, open to creativity on all sides, a level playing field that would provide enough space for anyone eager to exercise his God-given right to liberty, happiness, and economic advancement, opportunities galore to grow your business, as Tim might put it, wiser as he'd become to the advantages of free enterprise compared to government planning since his tour with HUD in Washington. And what they now brought to the table was a combination of Dad's broad experience and Tim's youthful enthusiasm, Dad the one to provide a concept, the boy the one to provide the necessary juice.

He had to acknowledge that it had been Tim's suggestion to place Princeton first on the sign, even if the lad, as a faithful Tarheel, didn't have any great love for the Ivy League. He said he knew that his name would soon be up there next to Dad's, and when that happened, depending on how and where things were progressing, they could rethink such minor priorities. But, he'd argued, from what he'd already learned in the business, it was best to keep things simple when you're moving into new country, use the name you've already established over time but exploit the known potential of your targeted territory. Smart kid.

Anyway, the change of the company name from Solar Properties to Solar Estates was his inspired revision, even if he had to say so himself about himself. Tim had always thought Solar a bit corny, his mother's soft-spoken contribution originally—dear Edith still the reticent type at fifty-eight—but Solar surely had its virtues, combining the benefits of the sun on this earth, including solar energy, with a higher aspiration that you didn't have to spell out in these high-flying days of solar system exploration. And Estates was clearly more appropriate than Properties for builders entering a town with the upscale history of Princeton and the resources of a clientele so unusually rich in possibilities, not least of all those related to real estate values.

Of course he wasn't ready to pretend that a family business could do more than exploit a small portion of those possibilities. You never wanted to over-promise and under-deliver. After all, Princeton wasn't Iraq, where some of his business buddies down south had made their small fortunes in reconstruction. His business was purely construction of model American homes, imaginative construction with all the bells and whistles, accompanied by studied landscape renewal. And he was happy to keep his strictly family business out to help other families prosper either as sellers or buyers, the bigger the consuming family the better, but whatever the size, the essential center of any project. So the prospects were good in a town that showed it had money to go along with its brains, some strong evidence of an ambition to hold its position of prominence halfway between New York and Philadelphia, land enough still to provide room for the kind of democratic expansion he and Tim had in mind.

But despite the obvious prospects, it would take effort, conviction, yes, even some courage in a town as sure of itself as this. He was ready, Tim was ready, what, after all, did they have to fear? As Tim would put it, the Good Lord was surely on their side. They had a second house almost ready, now this third lot, a more than two acre spread of mostly overgrown lawn and high trees—maybe a bit too high if the new owners went solar—and a reasonable chance to pick up the place next door given that small cinder-block Second World War curiosity in who knows what condition on the edge of what looked like an even larger lot. Anyway, it was almost time to head on over there and test the waters.

Cassie was not at all sure that she should be talking to this Randolph Parker of Solar Estates before Nick got home to be there as well, especially after driving by the new—what did they call these monstrosities, McSomething?—that this company had almost finished building on Independence Road, a horrible construction, as far as she was concerned, that looked as though it had been made of huge parts that didn't quite fit together three stories high on a mound of new earth that had been brought in to fill much of the original lot and raise the building so that it towered above all the homes around it at the end of the street like a mock castle built to protect some mad local celebrity from the threat of a violent mob.

This Randolph Parker must have heard that there were people in Queenston Park who were objecting to his latest giant intrusion, including several people in her own reading group who lived near it, some worried about facing more flooding problems when a building created so much of what they called run-off storm water and when the building ate up so much ground that used to absorb that kind of water. And there were others who didn't like the size of this McSomething so unlike anything else in that section of the Park, so out of proportion to what was around it and so arrogant in the space it took up on the street. And she and another lady she didn't know that well but who agreed with her about the shape of the building, how awful it looked with its great slanting windowless roof a story high above the second floor and a three-car garage sticking out of one side of it at an angle like a broken leg.

She had really done her best to put Mr. Parker off, but the man had been terribly persistent, very polite but ready with answers: her husband not being home wouldn't be a problem, he himself was only briefly in the neighborhood on business and needed no more than five minutes to explain on a preliminary basis his—how had he put it?—his current plans for developing the Queenston Park area, since a more detailed presentation of his mission could wait for a time when the whole family might be available to meet with him and maybe his family. And when she'd told him for no sensible reason that there was no longer a family here, her daughter Lydia lived in California with her own family, there was only her husband living here, the man had said, whatever, he'd just really be grateful if she could take five minutes of her time, etc. etc.

What did he really want? He may have heard that there were

complaints about all the huge buildings going up in the Township, letters in the local newspapers about the increased flooding problems, threats to the environment, etc., but he wasn't a politician making his case from house to house. That didn't really explain his persistence. Maybe he felt he had to add something to the sign he'd put up next door, play the good neighbor and report on what he had in mind, certainly nothing that was likely to please the eye or the heart if what he'd already brought into the neighborhood was the model. At least his voice had sounded fairly gentle, fairly quiet, even if there was something slippery about it. Anyway, what was five minutes in her life? Besides, she'd told him Nick might be back any moment, so—No such luck. From the window she watched the man coming up the front walk, older than she'd expected, gray-haired, slender, strong jaw, must have been handsome once. Firm touch on the doorbell.

"Cassandra. Randolph Parker. Randy for short. Not my favorite nickname, if you get my meaning, but that's the way it's been since high school."

"I'm Cassie for short. But I prefer Mrs. Mandeville when people don't know me. I'm old-fashioned that way."

"Right. Mrs. Mandeville is fine by me. Though I like the name Cassandra. Reminds me of some novel I read long ago. Can I come in?"

"Of course."

"Excuse the boots. I've been doing fieldwork in the area, so to speak. You have a terrific lot, I must say. Really terrific."

"That's the main reason we bought this house. To have space around us. And we hope we always will."

"I understand your feeling. You're not the first in this neighborhood to have worries about the future. All of us do in our way. I simply want to ask you for a chance to explain the role Solar Estates can play in securing that future."

"Well, I think both my husband and I would feel more secure if there weren't so much heavy building going on around us, including what you may have in mind putting up next door. According to some of the letters in our local newspapers, there isn't much thought among certain builders about the effect they have on flooding and on animal and plant life in our area. Not to mention open air to breathe."

"I can assure you, dear lady, that Solar Estates is very conscious of the impact of the environment on our efforts to raise the quality of real estate in this area. And I mean raise it not only environment-wise but aesthetic-wise."

"Well I've looked at the house you're building on Independence Road around the corner. I think it's monstrous."

"I'm sorry you feel that way. But I won't argue about it now. I just want to make arrangements to drop by and have a serious chat about what we're doing next door and hope to do in the future, as it may affect your future in a positive way. And without meaning to be pushy, the town's future as well."

"That house on Independence Road is just too big. Too big and too high on that great mound of earth you brought in, especially when most of the houses around it are small, ranch style, like this one. I'm sorry to say I don't think the house you built is a beautiful house. Three stories high with that huge roof, or is it more with a basement? And the three-car garage coming out at an angle as though a mistake in the planning."

"As I say, I won't make my case now. I don't want to go into specifics without the right documents in front of me. How about Sunday? In the afternoon? I'll have some plans to show you. And I'll bring my son along. Maybe my wife. They're a basic part of our mission."

"May I ask who was the architect of that house? I think you ought to reconsider using that architect."

"I was the architect, meaning I designed the model. But I promise not to take what you have to say personally. The truth is, I'm just as interested in sharing your ideas about what we might do down the road as I am about developing the lot next door."

"Down the road? How down the road?"

"Well, what I basically have in mind is your lot. It's even more interesting to us in a way than the lot next door because of the distance from here to the brook."

"My lot interests you? Our lot?"

"Well I'll save that for another day, Mrs. Cassandra. I mean Mrs. Mandeville. Please just keep an open mind till we have a chance to talk seriously again and I have a chance to lay out my concept, OK?"

Cassie didn't know what to make of Nick's new—what should she call it?—new hope for liberation. It didn't have to do with how he would spend his time on his sabbatical. That was his choice, and she had always kept what she felt was a proper distance from his work at home, his research and his writing, unless he himself brought her in by asking her to read something he'd written or asking her advice about the best way to answer some idiocy that had come his way or sometimes what a phrase really meant in a foreign language she knew better than he did— Americans were so limited that way, especially in Italian and French. She'd never intruded unless asked. But what he was asking her advice about now was really more serious. Choosing to retire at sixty-five, even if it was two years away and even if what he called "this new option" meant a supplement to his pension for going away early? Choosing to be free of what had been the focus of his life all these years? Their life?

Just why she felt it some kind of threat she couldn't be sure. Maybe it was the vagueness, the sense that he was looking for ways to escape, to find a new kind of freedom that wasn't clearly defined in his mind but that involved taking on a new way of life, more time for his own work, more time for travel whenever they chose, etc., etc. But he wasn't excluding her, so why was it in any way threatening? Maybe it had to do more with her than him, maybe any real change at that point in his life, in their life together, brought on some of the old insecurity that Nick had helped her challenge way back then, what she'd carried with her after she'd escaped Kavalla for Athens and then Athens for Rome, yes, what finally became something true for her even if it now sounded commonplace, a liberation from small-town attitudes, a broadening of horizons, etc., the virtues finally of a European-style education with some American teachers there for good measure. But along with that there was also the anxiety of being left alone to face those so-called brave new worlds, without any firm sense of place, sense of really belonging somewhere—this at moments had been hard to bear.

Until Nick came along. My God. Came along that first time asking permission to sit down opposite her at the outdoor table on the Gianicolo behind his American Academy where she'd come for a visit to learn what she could from a Fellows exhibition and had noticed him there, barely, a bit too old to be really interesting on first sight, though he had something boyish about him, dark curly hair, a loose-limbed way of walking that she had seen in other Americans, nice easy smile when she finally got close. Something of the boyish appearance and manner was still there, though the curly hair was thinner now, and gray had begun to take over what was left. It didn't matter. He kept himself reasonably trim, as she did, and there was more confidence in his walking, which was the exercise they shared. Anyway, back then he had apparently noticed her even more than she had noticed him, and he not only turned out to be ten years older than her but not as shy as he seemed at a distance, coming up to her that way at her table as though quite ready to sit down—how could she refuse him?—and more awkward than shy, having trouble getting his chair right so it wouldn't tip over as it almost did when he leaned way back to look casual. And she trying not to laugh, holding it to a smile, seeing him blush, then having to make up for that by talking too much about herself. And her English not yet good enough to be subtle even after a year at that American school.

Oh well. Maybe if she'd been more subtle with him back then, they never would have put together the next meeting and the meeting after that, and the final liberation. If that's what you could call it when it meant settling into another new community she knew not at all, becoming a kind of American housewife and mother—God knows, only a kind of—but with a house that was theirs on a piece of land that was theirs and nobody else's and in a town that, whatever else you might say about it, was more cosmopolitan than most and beautiful enough. After thirty years, it was simply home, the only real home now, and as far as she was concerned, harder and harder to leave even for part of the year. Especially now that she had made up her mind not only to fix up the backyard in its current rundown state but to take up gardening seriously. That would require some study, some serious planning, enough hard work so that she could create the kind of garden that might please her father, earn his pride when it was complete enough to be photographed and mailed to him for his pleasure. And Nick, with the free time he was planning to have, could surely help her with that—her own new liberation, if you will.

She heard the car turn into the gravel driveway. She still liked that sound. Time to relax. Time to meet him in the doorway and hug him to show she was glad to have him home.

"You just missed the man on the sign," Cassie said.

"Hello, dear girl. Come here. What man on the sign?"

"This Randolph Parker, Builder. He came by here a little while ago.

Came by for five minutes, I suppose to look us over. It was horrible."

"What was horrible? What did he do?"

"He didn't do anything. He was very polite. Maybe talked sometimes out of both sides of his mouth, but gently. The horrible thing is, he's not only taken over the place next door, he wants to take over ours as well."

"You're kidding."

"I'm not. He thinks our place is wonderful. It seems he likes it even better than the place next door."

"What does he like? If he buys our house, he'll tear it down."

"I know. It's our lot he likes. That's why it's horrible. He's the one who tore down the ranch house and built that huge thing on Independence Road. The one that has a tall black roof like a monk's hat and three garages jutting out of the side of it at an angle."

"What makes him think we want to sell our place? I haven't talked to anybody about that. Have you?"

"No. Why would I?"

"Well I just thought you might have, in general, because there's a lot of talk around about how valuable large lots still are in our area. And I suppose we'll have to think about it at some point."

"What point is that?"

"I don't know. Not anytime soon if I can help it. I mean if we're lucky. But nothing is forever. The point now is, I don't really like the idea of a builder snooping around our place, especially when we don't even know what he's up to next door."

"Well, he's ready to show us. He wants to come over on Sunday and lay out his concept."

"His what?"

"I don't know. Talk to us. Along with his family."

"His family? My God. And you agreed?"

"Well I didn't exactly disagree. Wasn't it the ancient Greeks who said know your enemy?"

As he studied the house, Randy was fairly certain that if he couldn't bring the Mandevilles around, his wife Edna could. She was simply a charmer, both in their social and business connections, her whole external personality changing shape when she came before people she wanted to persuade, whether friends or perfect strangers, as though nobody could be a threat, nobody unavailable to a proposition if she spoke with optimism and enthusiasm in the right language—and at least on the business side, she was really a master of the juicy phrase. Of course he knew the stubborn streak in her, the unchangeable opinions she held behind that sunny disposition, her superior attitude toward certain people, never Tim but sometimes toward their daughter-in-law Sheila and her friends, yet a priceless commodity when she confronted a consumer and spoke with all that positive thinking and commitment to values shining bright across her face. Of course, Sheila, also had her charm, what Tim had recognized as her creative imagination from the start, but Sheila wasn't as reliable as her Tim, sometimes flighty, not as sure of herself and therefore prone to fantasize, make things up to protect herself. But a good gal on the whole.

In the end Tim was proving to be the strongest of his helpers, maybe not always as convincing as his mother or as easy to read as his wife, but with a lot of self-assurance, a lot of faith in himself and what he thought was right by his God, even if that kind of faith sometimes failed to grip people and brought on a certain defensiveness which—without meaning to knock either his son or his president—reminded him of George W. when he wasn't at his best. At least both were in tune with higher aspirations, the drive to make things better for the piece of the world they controlled or hoped to control, so you could say the problem was really just a matter of surface presentation. Anyway, he was sure that underneath it all, there was no wavering in Tim's loyalty to the family business, its growth, its ongoing aims. He was really a relentless believer, and that was what showed through in the final analysis. Besides, he wouldn't be the one to do the talking when they spread their plans on the table. That was Dad's bailiwick first of all, with maybe an assist from Mom.

The problem was to find a convincing framework for making his case with the Mandevilles, hardly easy prospects if the wife spoke for both. He would begin by simply dealing with facts. Nobody could sensibly argue that a one-story Second World War house made of concrete block was important to preserve, even if the several floor-to-ceiling windows he'd spotted on the living room side suggested a somewhat advanced ranch style for its day. From the outside, at this distance, and even after his quick visit, he couldn't tell just how close the place was to falling apart, but after sixty years of that kind of construction and who knew what deterioration inside, it couldn't last all that long. And their lot was exceptional only in its size: more huge trees than it could manage, the brook at the back too far from the rear patio to be an aesthetic consideration, the whole spread of clay soil back there a potential flooding problem that only somebody with his experience really knew how to handle.

The trouble was, people weren't always rational about facts, and he understood that. They could be sentimental. He himself was sentimental sometimes, especially at movies that could bring him to tears, but he never let it come into his business negotiations if he could help it. He had the facts and he had the documents, all that should be needed to persuade this couple to join his forward-looking plans for making the neighborhood a model of democratic progress, territory that would include large families as well as small, those on the way up along with those retired, standard designs along with something more fashionable, housing both affordable and upscale, and so forth. The point was also to spread the profit, share it among buyer, seller, and builder in the progressive free enterprise way, the American way. In any case, he was sure Tim would see to it that things didn't turn too sentimental, just heartfelt enough to convince. He might be relatively young, but that boy was cool as a rock when it came to sentiment and shrewd enough to know its uses.

Time to gather his people from their tour of the new addition to Solar Estates—what a bonanza that mix of rotting timber and jazzed-up lawn turned out to be—and head over to the Mandevilles' for what might just become, God willing, another grand vista on the solar highway.

Cassie leaned over the dining room table and turned the plan sideways, then back again, then sideways again. She picked up the frontal-view sketch and studied it.

"It looks to me very much like the house on Independence Road," she said, still studying the sketch.

"Not exactly," Randy said. "There are the same number of bedrooms but somewhat smaller. And the garage you didn't like on that house is placed differently here. I'll show you."

He adjusted the plan and pointed at it to show her.

"It still looks like a three-car garage to me," Cassie said. "Though at least it isn't at an angle to the house."

"Well, whether three-car or two-car is still under negotiation. As is most everything else."

"But right up close to our border? And this parking lot spread out front? Where does the pollution go and the water running off?"

"The point of a garage is to cut down on pollution," Randy said. "It keeps the starting fumes under cover. And the parking plaza will be more or less permeable, I can guarantee."

"But six bedrooms? Who really needs six bedrooms in Queenston Park?"

"A lot of people, I'd say," Tim said. "Me for one. Me and my wife Sheila if we chose to settle in this part of town. By the way, she's sorry not to be with us but sends her best. Anyway, we plan to have children galore."

"That's good," Cassie said. "May they live for you."

"Huh?"

"That's what people say where I grew up. It's meant to be good luck for children."

"What a beautiful rug," Edna said. "Where is that rug from?"

"Turkey," Cassie said.

"Of course it is," Edna said. "How very exciting."

"What's happening here?" Nick said, drawing the plan in close. "It looks like a driveway heading to the back, right up against our border."

"Just a passageway," Randy said. "And not right up against your border. Be reasonable. Even the plaza's more than seven feet in, which is the Township regulation for structures. Besides, you'll be sheltered by a kind of wall along that passageway."

"Well," Cassie said. "Shall we say ten feet? That would allow our cat to go exploring just beyond our border until she runs into a wall. But not a deer. The deer would have to head downstream on the far bank of the brook to avoid the rush of water over here when the next hurricane arrives in town."

"I love the deer in this town," Edna said. "I'm not one of those who think they ought to be shot, even by arrows."

"Just how high will the wall over there rise above our border?" Nick asked. "It says five feet, if I'm not mistaken. But the visible house starts at three feet. Is that an eight foot rise?"

"No, just five foot," Randy said. "The ground floor will be about three feet above the parking plaza, more or less as it is now. So those three feet don't count."

"Well, they count in a sense," Nick said. "I mean if all you can see when you look out of here in that direction is cars parked in the air at about eye level."

"Excuse me," Tim said. "You exaggerate. Anyway, what do you see now when you look out in that direction? Just an old house on its last legs and a lot of unattended trees."

"Do you hear that, Nick?" Cassie said. "Just a lot of trees."

Edna came over and touched Cassie's hand. "I think maybe we ought to sit down quietly a minute and talk about our overall vision. Looking at plans too long can become very confusing. Besides, I'd be very grateful for a glass of water."

"And I'll take a beer if you have it," Tim said.

"Sure," Nick said. "I'll take care of that, Cassie. Anybody want anything else?"

"I'll have a scotch on the rocks," Randy said. "Just two rocks, OK?"

"Why don't all of you move into the living room and make yourselves comfortable," Nick said.

"Just one thing I'd still like to know," Cassie said. "If you put up a three-story house with a basement on a mound so close to our property line, how can we preserve our sense of open space? The thing will be hovering over us like a great shadow."

"But it will be a beautiful thing," Randy said. "Not like this thing next to you that's falling apart."

"And one thing we can guarantee," Tim said. "It will raise the value of your house beyond your dreams once you decide to sell."

"I know that might sound a bit commercial," Edna said. "What Randy and I have always emphasized is our vision of a neighborhood with people living next to each other in spacious new houses that provide more than mere easy living and that take full advantage of the above average space that lots in this area provide. It is a matter of quantity matching quality, of comfort matching vista, a harmonious way of living that you have earned the right to share with each other and the community."

"By watching a huge house go up next door?" Cassie said. "One that the papers say will cost over two million dollars?"

"No, by participating in our effort to help you make the most of what God has given you," Tim said.

Edna stared at him. "And in more down-to-earth terms, by participating in the upgrading of your neighborhood. You don't see it now, but no detail will be spared in what we'll provide next door. Everything will be mint-conditioned to meet the tenant's lifestyle needs, the décor of black and white warmed with wood finishes, all bathrooms with Thassos marble slab flooring, mosaic tile showers, and luxurious fixtures to make for a serene spa experience. What else? Hardwood-decked balconies out back and soaring ceilings to create a spatial environment quite grand compared to what a—what shall I call it?—a vintage ranch has to offer."

"Right," Randy said. "But to put it in even more specific terms, we hope you'll seriously consider a proposal we're ready to make that will relieve you of any worry about what we're planning to build next door."

"Ha," Cassie said. "Forgive me, but I think I know what you propose. You propose to buy our house and lot and have us move elsewhere."

"Not necessarily," Randy said.

"How not necessarily?" Nick asked, from the kitchen door.

"To put it in a nutshell," Randy said, "by building you a new house right here if that's what you'd prefer."

"For two million dollars?" Nick said.

"The price is negotiable," Randy said. "Like all things in life. But rest assured, we guarantee to provide you with a lot of space for the price point."

CHAPTER *Two*

Until this business with Solar Estates, Cassie hadn't taken the Queenston Park Housing Board seriously enough to think of approaching it regarding the question of what was permissible and what not in their presumably protected corner of Princeton, NJ. And she wasn't much encouraged by going over the restrictions listed in the Deed that all Queenston Park owners had to sign at the time of purchase and that Nick had dug out for her from his Home File. Even if one of the terms of the original 1940s deed that excluded "members of the Negro race" had been deleted because it had sometime since become against the law, others still appeared to her to be completely out-of-date or downright silly. Take the question of animals—as far as she was concerned, really rather elitist if not absurd: only dogs and cats and other household pets were officially allowed to live in the Park, everything else excluded, chickens and farm animals specifically. That must have come with the great upward transition from the odors of farmland to a gathering of lots restricted to white people during the Second World War. But at least no mention of squirrels and other rodents living there, and the deer and wild turkeys that visited regularly. Maybe these were really beside the point since the developers were sure to drive them away in time. And when it came to humans, only one family to a house? What about senior relatives such as the in-laws her sister had put up for years in her family home? What if, God forbid, Lydia got a divorce someday soon and moved back east to live with them, darling grandson Alex in hand?

She wondered if this 1940s document was influenced by what was left over in those days of her town's curious pre-Civil War association with the South. Anyway, she had to admit that some of the other Housing Board restrictions now seemed very much to the point, and she'd come to agree with the friendly neighbor—what was her name?—who suggested that she ignore the ridiculous items in the deed while being thankful for the non-ridiculous, which included no subdivision of any property however large the lot and no structure closer than thirty feet from a neighbor's boundary, parking plazas presumably not included. But what really irked her still was the clause in the deed that made clear the Board's duty to approve or disapprove the outside appearance of any new building or renovation.

Had they approved the appearance of the ghostly monster on In-dependence Road? Or had they been wearing blinders when they were presented the plans for that grand addition to the Park, with its crazy height and odd angles and dormer windows jutting out from the steep black-shingle roof that any child in the area was sure to see as the home of evil spirits just waiting for a chance to run wild through the neighbor-hood? Still, she had to say that in theory it was better to have that deed than no protection at all against the bad taste and pushy crowding and careless treatment of land that was beginning to take over the Park as one mega mansion after another priced in the millions rose up to replace—whatever. And her having given that curious '40s document a second reading at least succeeded finally, for what it was worth, in persuading her to get in touch with one of the current officers of the Housing Board to see what they might be planning to do about the ambitions of Solar Estates to cast a four-story shadow—if you counted the basement and dormered attic, and why wouldn't you?—over her still sunny and reasonably solid one-story ranch with nothing but a small patio out back to distract a neighbor's view of the tree-lined brook beyond.

What was it worth? No much in the end. She'd had to admit to Nick that the one Board officer she'd managed to get through to on the phone—obviously an old-time resident, but the voice strong enough—proved to be sympathetic: if he could help it, no more grand mansions by the builder she'd mentioned or any other without strict oversight by the Board, especially given the increased dangers from flooding in those sections of the Park where the brook sometimes got out of control. The trouble was, he'd said, most people in the region seemed indifferent, nobody really ready to take a stand. And then the Board itself was sometimes split between those on the one hand who felt owners ought to be free to handle their property as they pleased when it came to buying and selling, after all a privilege of democracy, and those on the other hand who favored stricter restrictions, even if the Board was finally limited in what it could try to enforce in view of the Township's softer restrictions—that is, short of going to court. Then again, when she'd asked rather too bluntly where the Board was when the plans were approved for that monstrosity on Independence Road, she could feel that the man had stiffened a bit at the other end of the line because he'd turned the thing right around and asked where the Mandevilles were when the plans were presented for review by Queenston Park owners.

What could she say? Traveling abroad with my husband as we often do when he's not teaching? She'd had to settle for telling the gentleman that he had a point, the Mandevilles should have been paying more attention when Solar Estates came into the neighborhood with its first huge building, but that still didn't explain the Board's approval of the latest monstrosity on Independence Road. This had changed the gentleman's voice again to something quieter: the Board had never seen the final plans, Solar Estates had piled in all that extra earth to create a great mound without their approval, though the builder must have had the approval of those in the Township administration who governed that sort of thing, which meant that there was nothing the Housing Board could do after the fact other than sue the builder, and that wasn't—how had he put it?—really practical.

So what were the absent Mandevilles to make of this now that they were facing a grand McMansion next door? The gentleman had suggested that the only thing to make of it was to take the question of building restrictions and flood regulations to another level, to the relevant meetings of the relevant committees and commissions and boards in the Township Municipal Building and a possible public discussion of the McMansion issue at the next meeting of the Township Committee itself, where the final power lay. Standing up to speak at such a meeting, he thought, would publicize the issue, a more effective strategy than the kind of informal discussions now going on among neighbors. Public airing of specific issues, controversial issues, was best for drawing in the press, he thought, and if anything could set local politics in motion, it was the press.

There you had it. Local politics. Where else would it be? Though she had no clear idea what that actually meant, how things actually worked locally in this great democracy that she'd come to admire even more than she admired what remained of its origins in her native country. Recently, of course, things over here no longer seemed as democratic as she'd once thought, at least not at the national level, but it would be interesting to see what went on at the local level to compare with questionable presidential elections and suspicious congressional maneuvering, probably not so different from what went on back in the home country. In any case, she was ready to learn, find out first of all what it meant to face the Township Committee if she could get up the courage to do that as the Housing Board member had suggested. Her most reliable teacher, her best support, surely had to be the one who'd brought her to Queenston Park in the first place and knew its still-curious connections to the past, if not yet exactly what it might have in store for their future. Could anybody really hope to know that from just looking out the window?

Though he felt the need for serious exercise, Nick decided not to take his usual walk by the lake path from Kingston into Princeton and back. Since the summer break for their trip to Italy, it had been months since he'd left the car at home and headed out into the neighborhood on the circular route that took him around the whole of Queenston Park, and even then he'd rarely given more than a glance to the mix of houses and mostly trimmed lawns he passed on his way, his mind elsewhere. This time he felt he had to pay more attention to what actually defined the borders of Queenston Park and what was inside them, specifically the damage from flood water reportedly caused by Harry's Brook coursing through territory made less permeable by excessive building. Where had he read that? *Town Topics*? *The Princeton Packet*? Anyway, with the goings-on next door, the huge construction planned, and the pressure he now felt to preserve the kind of lot and home he and Cassie had enjoyed all these years, it was important he know more about the territory Solar Estates was exploiting these days in a way that might not only complicate their future but the neighborhood's as well.

He also had to focus on helping Cassie confront the Township Committee at their next public meeting since that was what she now insisted she had to do, apparently not just because of her new interest in environmental issues but for her own inner satisfaction. How could he argue with that? And why would he? One thing she'd found out on her own was that the Committee was supposed to review the installation of new sidewalks in the streets leading to the Independence Road School, what Cassie's contact on the Queenston Park Housing Board had shrewdly suggested could be an occasion for bringing up the intrusion of the Solar Estates' new construction that had emerged to a height already tormenting some neighbors along that section of the Park. The gentleman, as she called him, had heard rumors that others in the neighborhood were planning to show up at the Township Meeting to protest. Great. Local democracy in action! Even if this was the first such rumored action by Queenston Park residents he'd heard about in all his years in the Township. But what did he know? During all those years he'd never been to a Committee meeting himself. Nor had Cassie.

Anyway, the research he'd managed so far seemed to confirm that those Committee meetings had room at some point for ordinary citizens to express their views not only on issues that appeared on the agenda but other issues as well, and if that was true, who knew what shared disgust might be brought into the open? Especially if there was follow-up in the press. Cassie was already ahead of him on that score. He'd realized how important this whole thing was to her when he'd offered to speak at the meeting in her place if she ended up feeling too nervous about it, and she'd given him that over-my-dead-body look: "That's sweet of you, my love, but I think I can deal with it. I have to learn to deal with it."

Good. But he didn't want to be shut out, he wanted to help. The issue was his as much as hers. He'd have to do more research, find someone who could tell him what really went on at those meetings, maybe get some literature from the Township Municipal Building. Strange not to know anything about that aspect of living in the Township. Meetings were announced somewhere, surely online, questions were asked and presumably answered, decisions were made, and your participation, just about everybody's participation as far as he could tell, was reading about it in one or another of the local newspapers sometime in the days that followed.

As he turned east off Independence Road, he pushed himself to focus on the layout: the lots suddenly much narrower on one side of the road, houses set back more or less in line, just about every mid-century style there at the pleasure of the first owner, from ranch to split level to colonial to white-brick cottage to cinder-block original, even to miniature castle gothic. There was something exhilarating about the eccentricity of the last, the free-wheeling expression of some adult child—exhilarating until you came to the sign in front of the house next door, a single-story double-length ranch with a partial brick façade: Capital Builders? Out of Trenton? Was the old motto "Trenton Makes the World Takes" moving north to begin a new life in Princeton along with the juvenile gangs that had begun to come in from that region for dangerous fun and games on the paths below the high school? And just one house, a large two-story colonial, separating the Capital Builders from another new sign: Keystone Mansions, Lawrenceville and Princeton? Christ Almighty. Overwhelming. In less than six months? And across the way, the first of the two Solar Estates in Queenston Park, no doubt the top-heavy model for what would rise in glory four stories high next door to their one-story cinder-block experiment from the '40s. Where would such progress stop? Could it possibly be stopped? It really had to be, somehow.

Thinking back on it, Cassie had to admit that the lady behind the information desk in the Township Municipal Building had really been quite patient with her, speaking slowly, softly, though her face had a rigid smile almost from beginning to end, as though put a bit on the defensive by the tone of the questions she had to deal with. How the lady had educated her! She was honestly sorry, she'd said, but even though Cassie was a voting citizen, she couldn't simply put an item on the Township Committee agenda because it happened to be of special interest to her. And the lady had patiently explained that items on the agenda were matters of official business determined in advance by the Township after study and review of decisions taken and recommendations made by various sub-committees and commissions and boards appointed by the Township and working under the Township Committee, such business calling in the end for a vote by Township Committee members only, not by ordinary citizens. And when asked whether that was truly a democratic procedure since she, Cassandra Mandeville, ordinary citizen that she was, didn't belong to any commissions or boards in the Township, the lady had pointed out, still more or less gently, that of course the five Township Committee members were elected representatives of you and me, what could be more democratic? Besides, any citizen had the right to attend public meetings and speak his or her mind, an essential aspect of democracy in America called free speech.

She'd wanted to ask the lady if that meant free speech only on agenda items or on any item of community interest, as Nick seemed to think, but she could sense that the lady's patience was running thin by then, no doubt assuming from the remnants of a foreign accent hovering in front of her that she was dealing with a politically illiterate alien. In any case, whatever was on the agenda, Mrs. Cassandra Mandeville, long since ordinary citizen of the United States if resident alien once upon a time, would be at the next meeting of the Township Committee and she would speak her mind, you could bet on it. The only way they would stop her was by tying her up and putting tape across her mouth, like in the movies, or maybe just a silk scarf, the way the more genteel junta interrogators in Greece preferred to silence women suspects who protested too much back then during the dictatorship.

Counting on this democratic option of speaking in public had finally made it easer for her to accept Nick's suggestion that it would be politic—weren't those his words?—to go along with the new overture from Solar Estates to meet *en famille* again so that Randy Parker could rectify what he'd called an apparent failure of communication between them, a confusion about objectives, a misunderstanding of shared prospects, she couldn't remember what else, all of it sounding, Nick said, as though it should be in capital letters. Overture? OK, but what she really expected from this second visit by the Parker family was some sort of shady proposition that would prove a waste of time. Anyway, when Nick explained that by politic he meant having another chance to see exactly what they were dealing with, she felt she had to agree, especially after he reminded her that she herself had said you should give your opponent—enemy is what she'd actually said—every opportunity to reveal himself. How could she object? And it certainly wouldn't be a waste of time if she and Nick ended up seeing their opponent wearing the same mask.

The bell. Twice? Why twice? Solar Estates could just wait a minute while she got Nick to come in from his study. She'd spotted three of them over there casually surveying the spread of their new acquisition on the far side of the property line, one of them a younger woman who looked to be in her early thirties, petit, ash-blond chin-length hair, in a navy suit with matching two-tone pumps who must be Tim Parker's wife, walking the lot down to the brook without more than a glance at the house they would soon bring down, and now on this side of the border no doubt ready to report that there were no barbarians over there if you chose to look at things through the right kind of rosy glasses. Ha.

"Just a minute. I'll get my husband. Come in and make yourselves comfortable."

"Mrs. Cassandra. Cassie. Hi. I want you to know how much Tim and Sheila here appreciate your giving us another chance to—right. I'll wait for your husband to join us."

Sheila thrust out her hand. "I'm really pleased to meet you, Mrs. Cassandra. I've heard so much about you. It's thrilling to know that we'll be neighbors. In a manner of speaking. For a while, anyway."

Cassie took her hand. Sheila clung to it, and smiled. Cassie saw that Sheila chose her jewelry as carefully as her clothes, a gold bracelet on her wrist, a pearl necklace with a gold clasp at the neck, and on her left hand, a ring set with a large solitaire diamond.

"I think it's important for neighbors of whatever kind to start off on the right foot," Sheila said. "Share as much of their faith as they can, know where they're coming from, don't you think?"

Cassie broke free. "I hear my husband stirring. It just takes him a minute to finish a sentence or shut down the computer or whatever. Have a seat. All of you."

"I feel I may have given you a wrong impression last time I was here with Mom and Dad," Tim said to her back. "I'd like to make up for that by putting my thoughts right on the table."

"Hello," Nick said from the dining room. "Feel free. Let's have your thoughts. And we'll give you ours. Which is why we're here."

Randy stretched out a hand. "Maybe before we get into our general philosophy I'd like to—"

"Sorry, Dad, this is important to me. As Sheila said, I want these good people to know from the start where we're coming from. I know you think ours is a commercial enterprise and it is, I won't deny that, but it is a progressive one. It involves a commitment to change, to betterment, values that I learned and embraced even under the stress of restrictions while I was working for the government in Washington. And it involves a full sharing in the benefits that progress will bring to each of us in this quality neighborhood. Let me be specific."

"Tim, boy. Sorry. I'll do the specific. You round out the concept and the vision."

"May I say something?" Sheila said. "I mean before the men get involved in the serious side of things? You'll understand, Mrs. Cassandra. We're a family. You're a family. We're on our way to having children just as you've had already. We think about our future just as you do. I mean, we have so much in common from the start that transcends almost all other considerations. So much shared life. I just want this out there in front of us before we get into the business side of things."

"Right," Tim said. "But let me just say that our vision may certainly be seen as the serious side of things, and it is, but it's still relatively simple if absolutely essential. The houses in Queenston Park, most of them, are now more than fifty years old. Some of them are already falling apart, others will follow shortly. The lots, on the other hand, are exceptionally large, most of them, three-quarters of an acre to three acres. Land in this town is at a premium. Is it worth preserving dilapidated houses on lots as large as these, as valuable as these, in a prime real estate region that is becoming more and more—"

"You think our house is dilapidated?" Cassie said.

"Excuse me, I didn't say that. I was trying to express a broader perspective. Some houses on some lots. Anyway, my point is that the true value of your property is not being realized under current circumstances. It is our vision to see you and others in this community taking advantage of what God has given you, namely the incredible appreciation in the value of the real estate you own as fortunate citizens of this high value town, while we the builders—here is the true sharing—provide you the prospect of your special residence in an iconic style, the most comfortable, luxurious, modern living you could want should you choose to join us.

Cassie smiled broadly, stiffly. "And this you do by tearing down our comfortable house and building a giant monstrosity in its place?"

"Oh," Sheila said. "I can't believe what I'm hearing."

"Monstrosity is a matter of opinion," Tim said. "Elegant grandeur would be my way of putting it. Anyway, we don't force you to live in the house we would build. You can sell us your property and live anywhere you want to, or you can let us build a house on your property and we—"

"Let me clarify," Randy said. "As I tried to explain last time we were here, living in a house we would build on your lot is simply an option, one in which you could participate with full freedom of choice. You want three bedrooms or four instead of five, that's fine by us. Or you want a two-car garage instead of three-car garage, fine. Certainly you would want something more than a carport. So we can buy the lot from you or we can build a house on your lot at our reduced rate and you can live in that house or sell it for a profit and make arrangements to live elsewhere, which we would be happy to help you arrange. All options are open."

"Let me ask you one thing," Nick said. "Why is it so important for you to build on our lot? Is it because of what you're planning to do next door?"

"Only in the broadest sense," Randy said. "It would certainly help our rehabilitation program to have two houses in a row on two such generous lots as a cornerstone of our progressive neighborhood enterprise. I'm being absolutely honest."

"May I add, to put it simply, that it would have symbolic value?" Sheila said.

"Right, or what might better be called emblematic value," Tim said.

Sheila turned in her chair to stare at him.

"But why does this house you're building next door have to be so tall and so close to ours?" Cassie said. "What's the symbolic value in that?"

Sheila turned back to frown at Cassie, head tilted.

"I'll be frank," Randy said. "It's partly a question of conforming to appropriate restrictions. There's only so much space you're allowed to build on in this area. I mean, there are essential environmental concerns, specifically wetland and flooding issues, and we plan to be as sensitive environmental-wise as we possibly can be."

Cassie gave her smile again. "I think I know something about those issues. I've heard from neighbors that there's a serious problem of flooding in the Park downstream from us. And even our lot's been flooded by overflow from Harry's Brook twice during hurricane time. How does this huge house you're planning to build next door or the one you're planning to build here avoid increasing the flooding problem?"

"That's an easy one," Randy said, reaching down for the worn leather folder he's set against a table leg. "I have some material here I'd be happy to show you relating to both design and wetland issues that I think may meet anybody's lifestyle needs while being environmentally friendly."

"I don't think this is the right time for that," Nick said. "We're just not ready yet—"

"Does the design have the same steep roof?" Cassie asked. "The pointed gables? The great hill of earth? The garages jutting out on one side at an angle?"

"It's a serious variation of our basic design, Mrs. Mandeville. Trust me."

Sheila crossed her legs. "Trust is everything. It's as simple as that."

"Look," Nick said. "Let's not waste anymore of your time. We're not ready to discuss options and we're not ready to look at new plans, right Cassie? If and when we are, we'll be back in touch, OK?"

"No problem," Randy said. "We have all the time in the world. Beautiful Queenston Park is here to stay and to grow and I assure you Solar Estates will be staying and growing right along with it in the months and the years ahead."

The Township Committee meeting room reminded Cassie of the courtroom in Salonika that she'd visited with her father as part of her tour of that city long enough after the civil war and before the Colonels' coup to have made an innocent visit of that kind plausible. Here as there, she faced a raised platform at the front of the room where the presiding authorities would sit in a row—judges there, Committee members here—and a bit of platform at the side for what looked like the perch of an official secretary or clerk of some kind, a long table below for administrative personnel, a small table on its own for a lady of broad shoulders and flowing amber hair preparing to start her recording machine, and the seats for those admitted to the proceedings laid out like a classroom. All that was missing from this room was the walled-in section at the side where jurors would sit, obviously unnecessary here since, as far as she knew, nobody came here to be tried even for traffic violations. So why did she feel as though she'd come to this place to defend herself? It was clearly her fault that the room felt strangely familiar. She'd never been here before, she didn't know how things proceeded, where was the threat? But she still didn't feel comfortable enough to tell Nick what she was feeling. It really didn't make sense.

Nick turned back from the center aisle podium and handed her a copy of the Township Committee agenda, then slouched down beside her to read through his. Almost all the items on the agenda looked new to her, most of them presumably initiated sometime before she began to follow newspaper accounts having to do with local real estate issues. There were at least twelve items under "Consent Agenda: Contains items of routine nature, which are approved by a single vote." There was one "Ordinance Public Hearing," and seven "Ordinance Introductions." She tried to read all of them conscientiously, but only one item really woke her up: "*An Ordinance Concerning Alcoholic Beverage Consumption in Public Places and Urinating in Public Places and Amending the 'Code of the Township of Princeton, New Jersey, 1968.'*" She checked that item with her pencil, added a question mark, and passed her agenda to Nick.

He smiled, made a face, then took her pencil and checked the fourth general category on her agenda: "Comments from the Audience." That, he turned to tell her, was supposedly where she could make the statement they'd rehearsed, though it wouldn't do any harm if both of them tried to pay attention to what was going on before that as a learning experience in local democracy, however boring. She mumbled "Democracy. O.K. But what kind of democracy is it when you have an agenda this long and you can't even get an item on it as an ordinary citizen?" He smiled: "You've got a point," then patted her knee.

The five-member Committee filed into their places on the platform from a door in the wings: a thin woman with tinted white hair, a late-middle-aged man with a gray beard and an open collar, a younger black man in a navy-blue suit and red tie, a middle-aged woman with dull blond hair and a purple flower in her jacket lapel, finally the Mayor, shortest of the men, thick white hair, smiling flushed face, a goatee like an arrowhead on his chin. He was followed by two sober-faced men in jackets and ties who sat down behind nameplates for Township Attorney and Township Administrator.

The Mayor looked very cheerful, adjusted himself in his seat at the center of the platform, glanced right and left and asked that his companions make sure they had their microphones at the proper level behind their name plates. He smiled broadly at the audience of nine and moved without preface into the "Consent Agenda," reading out each resolution in a strong bass voice, pausing to see if any Committee member had a question. Since they were all so-called routine items that Nick told her had been through some sort of review by some lower committee or board, there were only a few technical questions from the Committee members on this or that item before the Mayor asked the clerk to call the vote. There was a loud "Yes" five times, ending with the Mayor, who then paused at the request of the recording secretary while the vote became part of the official record.

Cassie leaned toward Nick. "So quick? So unanimous? Is that why it's called the Consent Agenda?"

"Could be," Nick said. "Anyway, the Committee members, including the Mayor, elect the Mayor, so they start off with certain consent."

"You mean the people don't elect the Mayor?"

"Five of the people. Just not including you and me and everybody else in the Township who isn't a Committee member."

The Mayor was reading the next item under the title ORDINANCE PUBLIC HEARING, a bond ordinance authorizing, as a local improvement, a sidewalk on the north side of Coolidge Lane, the authorization to include an assessment to the residents of 50 percent of the cost. The Mayor reported that the residents had opted for blacktop rather than cement to reduce the cost of the assessment, which would be proportioned as usual on the basis of lot frontage, and since the ordinance had been approved by vote after its introduction at the previous Township meeting, the second vote at this time would be final. Any discussion? No response. Any questions? An ancient man—face deeply lined, arms thin, only a wisp of hair—stood up and made his way slowly to the microphone at the podium in the center aisle.

"Harry Sims, your honor. My question: why do we need a sidewalk on Coolidge Lane? I don't need a sidewalk. It's supposed to be for children going to school. I don't see any children on Coolidge Lane. All of us have at least one foot in the grave."

"Thank you, Mr. Sims," the Mayor said. "And please don't refer to me as your honor. I'm not a judge. I'm just an elected official trying to do my duty with too little time on my hands. Any further questions?"

Mr. Sims returned to his seat. A blonde lady wearing white slacks and a pink blouse with one button open at the neck stood up and walked to the podium with a firm stride. "Your honor, I for one—"

"Your name, please?"

"Nora Gadjusek. Excuse me. I for one expressed my displeasure to one of the people working for the Township Engineer when they came into our neighborhood. I forget his name. Anyway, I expressed my displeasure about a sidewalk on a road already too narrow. Others did too. So how can you say the residents opted for this or that? Some of the residents, maybe. But who is to know how many?"

"The Clerk knows how many," the Mayor said. "You're welcome to have a look at the record anytime. As a matter of fact, I encourage you to do that. Any further questions? Comments by members of the Committee? Comments by others? If not, I call the vote."

The members voted "Yes" in turn.

"We move on now to Ordinance Introductions," the Mayor said. "The first of these has to do with the addition of sidewalks on Union Avenue where it enters the Township from the Borough. There has been a certain controversy about whether to extend the current Borough sidewalks on both sides of the street or just on one side. The proposed ordinance calls for both sides. I understand that Committee member Morris would like to speak on the issue. Mr. Morris."

Mr. Morris leaned forward in his chair and adjusted his microphone. "As the only person of color on this Committee, I feel I have a special obligation to object to this ordinance in the first instance. It is ridiculous. The Borough side of the neighborhood in question, once affordable by those of us who have lived in the vicinity for some generations, I may say beginning well before the Civil War, is already taxed beyond the means of most newcomers. Buying in on the Township side has proven to be a way of surviving for some of us, but extending the sidewalks into that area would simply burden those of us who have managed to keep ahead of the growing cost of living in this beautiful but expensive town. Sidewalks on this side or that? I say no sidewalks at all, at least not this year or the next. If we want sidewalks, I suggest we solicit our friends in the Borough to replace those now crumbling in the old neighborhood. And I suggest we pay more attention to the honeycomb of potholes in Union Avenue on the Township side."

"Thank you, Mr. Morris. Any more questions?"

There were no more questions. The Clerk called the roll of members. The ordinance passed 4 to 1.

The Mayor took up the next item, an ordinance authorizing sewer lateral repairs.

Cassie looked at Nick. "How can they just vote like that and move on to the next item? I think that Committee member had a point."

"Of course he had a point. And I guess the others feel he had a chance to make it, so that is that. Local democracy. Anyway, the ordinance comes up for a second vote at the next meeting, not that I think the vote will be any different."

"I just don't understand."

"Shush" came from behind. Cassie turned to look. The man behind her was staring straight ahead at the podium. He was twiddling a pencil over the pad of paper in his lap. Cassie turned back and sat there with her head bowed. She began to wonder who would bother to listen when she got up to speak, what difference would it make with so few ordinary citizens in the audience? At least one of them was obviously a reporter. Who were the others? She didn't recognize any of them. Why were they really there? She felt ignorant, an outsider, about to make a fool of herself by saying things of no importance to anybody else. She felt Nick's hand patting her knee again, then holding firm.

The Mayor was providing the background to the ordinance concerning alcoholic beverage consumption and urinating in public places: a lady had called the Township police to complain that she had spotted a group of men, no less than five, behaving in a rowdy, drunken manner at the edge of the restaurant parking lot on the border of her lawn, in fact suddenly lining up to urinate in some kind of sequence that suggested a competition. She was distressed, disgusted. Two squad cars were dispatched to apprehend the perpetrators, and though it became clear they had been drinking at some sort of reunion event in the restaurant next door to the lady's townhouse, they were not exactly drunk, and they reported that they had been forced to leave the restaurant and use what they called "outside facilities" because the men's room facility in the restaurant had broken down earlier that evening. They claimed they were innocently celebrating long-standing fellowship. After verifying the condition of the toilet at the restaurant, the attendant police released the men without charge, but at a subsequent review of the circumstances, the Committee had determined that the Township Code should be amended to cover episodes of this and related kinds.

The mayor now read out the revised text: "'No person shall urinate or place any bodily waste of humans on any public street, sidewalk or other place in public view, or to which the public is invited or has access, except in a lavatory toilet or similar facility.' Any questions?"

The younger of the female Committee members had a question. She leaned forward to her microphone: since she had been unable to attend the meeting that reviewed the complaint, she would like to know whether the revised code was intended to apply equally to men and women. When the laughter subsided, the Mayor said that he assumed the words "person" and "humans" applied to both sexes. Less laughter. The vote was called: unanimous in favor of the ordinance.

The Mayor stood up and suggested that it was time for a ten-minute comfort break, no joke intended.

Cassie laid her head on Nick's shoulder.

"Tired?" he asked. "We don't have to stay any longer if you don't really feel like it."

Cassie sat up straight. "I want to stay. I—never mind."

Nick took her hand. A woman's voice behind them mumbled to her companion: "I wish our woman mayor hadn't retired. Some people didn't trust her, but now and then she showed she had a heart. And she wasn't silly. At least not regularly."

When the Mayor returned, he said that since some in the room were apparently getting restless, and time was indeed flying, he'd decided to take only a moment to report briefly and unofficially on the overflow of Harry's Brook in the aftermath of the recent storm, an issue that had raised a certain concern in the press and elsewhere. Cassie leaned forward to listen. Nick leaned forward beside her. The Mayor reported that the overflow had been limited, the flooding soon under control, and there had been only minor damage to property in the Township. He said in any case he wanted it known that Harry's Brook was a continuing issue that the Committee would return to in due course. Someone in the audience groaned loudly. The Mayor looked up from his papers, flickered a smile. "I assume that is meant to anticipate the next item on the agenda, Comments from the Audience. Please raise your hand if you have something useful to say."

Cassie felt Nick nudging her. She raised her hand along with several others. The Mayor chose a gray-haired man wearing a light blue shirt and neat blue jeans, with a blazer draped over one shoulder. At the center aisle podium the man introduced himself as Professor Somebody or Other, glanced at some notes, adjusted the microphone.

"My comment has to do with the castle of seven gables that the builder called Solar Estates is in the process of completing on Independence Road. I have one of the lots that is adjacent to this newly developed addition to our once relatively amiable, even intimate community, and I have watched the mansion next door grow from a vast hole in the ground to the grand three-story structure plus a basement on a newly created high mound of earth presumably waiting for a moat to be dug around it. This huge creation replaced my recently deceased neighbor's modest one-story home on a reasonably flat piece of land with ample trees, garden, open space from its neighbors, etc. As the new mansion rose to its full height, I felt myself creeping lower and lower inside my two-story cottage below it, found myself spending more and more time in my ground-floor living room, even sleeping there sometimes when insomnia from a mild form of agoraphobia became increasingly intense— that is, a fear of being swallowed by huge people suddenly appearing in the world outside my window."

The professor looked down, cleared his throat, raised his head elegantly. "Though the new house next door was then barely complete, my wife began to draw the shades in our upstairs bedroom even during daylight hours to avoid the gaze of whoever might be over there looking down on us from their second and third story windows high up on their man-made hill. I ran into our neighbor living on the backside of this grand construction, and it was clear that he too had begun to suffer from an anti-voyeur syndrome and me-much-smaller-than-you complex brought on by this overbearing intrusion into our once unpretentious neighborhood. In short, Solar Estates should go fly a kite."

Pause. The Mayor: "Is there a question in all this?"

"Yes. Yes indeed. Put simply, why oh why has the Township allowed this abomination to rise to such an intimidating height on a mound of earth that has filled much of the lot next door to mine and thus created a persistent threat of flooding, while also serving to uproot trees that were once good for many a green thought in a green shade, replacing these with walls and windows more than high enough to challenge the privacy of my wife of many years while at the same time humbling her husband's stature?"

The Mayor looked to his right and left. "Is any Committee member prepared to answer the question?"

No Committee member was prepared to answer the question, but someone at the staff table representing the Township Engineering Department picked up a microphone to say that, after serious negotiations, Solar Estates had finally met all necessary requirements at that particular site.

A woman on the other side of the room stood up. "Including the trees cut down? The flooding problem?"

"Yes, including the trees and the flooding problem. New trees will be planted; runoff pipes will provide proper drainage into the local system. Given the particular wetland situation there, a certain height was required—"I don't understand how that—"

"Your name, please," the Mayor said.

"Forget it," the woman said. "It's obviously too late to do anything about the way that lot's been decimated. It's simply a scandal. And whoever in the Township administration approved it ought to be ashamed."

"I second that," came from another voice.

"Please," the Mayor said. "If you want to speak, raise your hand to be recognized and come to the podium microphone to say your name. We can't have unidentified voices from all over the place."

"Ah," said a loud voice. "The truth will out, microphone or no."

"The truth will out, shouted down or no," the Mayor said. "Hands please?"

Cassie raised her hand, was motioned forward, stood up, paused, eased past Nick who gave her waist a pat, then made her way up the aisle to the podium. She hesitated, took a deep breath.

"Cassandra Mandeville from Queenston Park. I have to say at the start that I'm not really familiar with this kind of local democracy, but I'm truly trying to believe in it. I have been in this country and this town for over thirty years and I have lived with my husband in the same house for most of those years, but this is the first time I'm attending a meeting of the Township Committee. So I am not sure what is the best way to say what I want to say."

"Could you speak a little closer to the microphone," the Mayor said. "We up here have barely heard a word."

"Yes, I am shy in front of a microphone, I have to admit that. But I am also angry, so I will be pleased to raise my voice. I don't understand how this Township can allow a builder from I don't know where to come into our neighborhood and build a thing as big and ugly as what is now on Independence Road. But I won't speak about that because others who live closer to that house than I do have already spoken their mind."

"I'm afraid you're still too far from the microphone," the Mayor said.

"All right. Is this loud enough? Thank you. What I and my husband Nick behind me over there have come here to question are the plans by the builder Solar Estates, who says he has your approval, to raise another huge—I don't know what to call it, McMansion as the newspapers call these things?—anyway, a huge house with three stories of walls and windows and an elevated driveway leading to I don't know how many garages opposite our one-story ranch house, and all this only ten feet or so from our border. Have you been able to hear this?"

"Yes, yes," the Mayor said. "Calm yourself."

"I will try to be calm. But how can I be calm? I don't know how high this construction will rise above the earth, but from what I have seen of the plans, it looks as though the first floor of three floors will begin half way up the level of our living room because it will have a basement under it hidden from the front. Anyway, it is as though we will become the servant quarters to some god-like giants, maybe gentle giants, but grand enough to frighten us out of our home so the builder can raise another huge construction on our land in place of our simple house. Excuse me for my bad way of speaking. When I am angry I sometimes lose my normal way of speaking and start to become—what shall I say?—something Homeric."

"That's all right," the Mayor said. "Just try to relax. But please come to your question."

Cassie glanced back at Nick. He gave her an OK sign with thumb and forefinger.

"My question. Yes. The point is, this gentleman builder assures us that he has met your requirements for the house he plans to build next to ours, just as he has met the requirements for the huge house on Independence Road. And he would be pleased to buy our house and our lot so that he can build another house maybe even bigger than the one about to block us from the sun on one side, block us from some of our open sky. So, my question. What is the point of requirements that allow this sort of—what shall I call it?—this sort of greedy invasion of our neighborhood? Houses so high on earth brought in and raised so close to other houses? Houses made up of what are described as modules nailed on top of each other and beside each other in a style that—let me try to be courteous—that ends up no more than common, uninspired, or worse. Trees cut down and drains buried in their place, I mean really. Please, I ask you, help me as an ordinary citizen who was adopted by your country long ago, please help me to understand why after many good years in this town I now seem about to lose some of the open space to the sky and the pleasures of green all around that have made me feel free here as nowhere else in the world. Thank you."

The Mayor turned to the Committee. "Would anyone care to answer the good lady?"

The older, white-haired female Committee member pulled her microphone close. "It seems to me in view of what has been said here tonight that there is reason to review the restrictions now in place to see if they are still serving the whole community as they should. I will call for such a review at the appropriate time."

"Yes," the Mayor said. "I would support that course of action. A review. But let me add one thing. There are two sides to this issue. The side that has not been represented here tonight is that of home owners who have sold their houses to the builder in question or to other builders and who have a right, as property owners, to do what they choose to do with their property. That is also an aspect of democratic freedom."

The Mayor paused. Three hands went up. He ignored them.

"A review of restrictions must take the interests of these citizens into account as well. And in a town where real estate values are as high as they are here, Borough or Township, some home owners have every reason to take advantage of the appreciation in their property that has come to them during the years since they moved into our community. In this respect, they can be grateful to the developer who offers them an opportunity to realize that appreciation, whether short term or long term. I say this just to put our discussion in proper perspective. In simple language, there are two sides to this issue as there are to most, and both sides must be respected. Any more questions or comments?"

Silence. Cassie returned to her seat. Nick was smiling stiffly. He leaned over to whisper, "Well, that sure killed further debate. At least for the time being. But you did well. Really. You should be proud."

"I'm not proud. I'm still confused. I feel I'm inside a wall somebody has built around me and I can't find a way through it."

"We'll find a way," Nick said.

A man wearing a light windbreaker who looked as though he could still be an undergraduate except for a gray-streaked beard the length of his hand was now at the microphone asking for more attention to the problem of bicycle lanes. Several people got up to leave, and with a nod of the head Cassie signaled to Nick that she was ready to go. In the corridor outside the meeting room, a woman with a folder in one hand, blond hair reaching her shoulders, came up beside Cassie and touched her arm. "Don't sell your house. I mean don't give in to that builder yet. There are ways to fight him."

CHAPTER

Three

R andy Parker turned into the driveway by the boathouse and parked where he could have a clear view across the lake at the stretch of forest between the lakeside and the canal somewhere beyond it. Not that there was anything to look at, no houses over there, but he wanted a few minutes without distraction to settle his mind for the case he planned to make at the engineering office in the Township Municipal Building. What Tim had done to complicate things still bothered him, but he doubted that would make much difference with the professionals in charge of serious business over there. If necessary, he would explain that it hadn't been his idea to respond to the newspaper report on the Township Committee meeting in the way Tim had, with all those quotes so critical of what Solar Estates was trying to do for the neighborhood in question. The lad had simply lost his cool, in the end forgivable for someone his age. His own policy was not to answer public criticism, let it just die its slow peaceful death, and to confront such critics only by the kind of positive presentation of the family business—with all the bells and whistles, as Sheila would put it—that could fit into their standard ad, highlighted by a photo of the two generations of Parkers in a sunny mood.

He picked up the newspaper on the seat beside him. OK, so Tim had a different approach, and the house on Independence Road was his project, but if he and Edna hadn't been out of town, they would have been there to help out when the reporter tracked Tim down, been there to put in a word every now and then to keep the playing field level. What got into print was really too much. Christ Almighty, just the headline, MCMANSION BUILT ON FILL-IN HILL MAKES NEIGHBORS BOIL, was enough to make you shiver. Even more so, Tim's line about these misdirected people who were typical Princeton residents against any kind of change. Typical residents? Some you were hoping would become your clients? Not much subtlety there. And not much subtlety calling their complaints all emotion and little reason, let alone calling all their homes in that neighborhood in need of repair and mostly difficult to market. Even if that was largely true. But do you say that to a reporter? And what must have pissed off the nosiest complainers was this off-the-wall line about who wants to live in a one-story 2000-square-foot house?—not very smart when you're moving into a neighborhood that's surrounded by one-story houses with that kind of footprint. He could just see the Greek lady turning purple on reading that particular remark: "Exactly the kind of house I want to live in since that's what I've been living in for thirty years."

It came down to a matter of strategy. Criticize your potential clients, even if you think them your enemies, and you end up sounding defensive. If you're going to take a stand when you know you're right, don't let your guard down and keep on the offensive. In short, go for the positive, like, for example, our company is attempting to combine traditional elegance with cool modernity in architectural design at a cost that should satisfy any seller or buyer who has advanced taste along with a sense of his or her earned rewards. The his or her is of course essential these days. If Tim didn't get that, Sheila would get it for him. That girl knew what it meant to be politically correct when it came to the female species, and she also knew how to stay on the offensive.

It was too bad the two of them seemed to have trouble figuring out how best to fit into the family business, how to work together rather than in some kind of secret competition. Not that they were exactly at each others throats all the time, just too tense with each other when it came to important decisions. Had she been with him when that reporter turned up she might have helped him tone down that interview, or maybe tone it up the right way, that is, go for the jugular but only when necessary. Though looking at it strictly from Tim's point of view, you couldn't find all that much room to respond politely to people quoted as labeling his Independence Road project either despicable or ugly or—get this—oppressively dominant.

Maybe the best you could do was write a letter to the editor in a more or less conciliatory tone, simple language, simple truth, something about your not having intended to offend anybody with your comments in an interview you hadn't solicited, your intention being merely to point out that there is a demand for luxury homes in Princeton, New Jersey, and good market opportunities for most anybody living there. And maybe something about your company's history of being available to open discussion of options, of new ideas, of workable requests from neighborhoods, since the mission that guides Solar Estates is community improvement in the American way of responsible free enterprise in a democratic society governed by reasonable regulations. No, reasonable laws rather than regulations—broadens the issue, makes it more than a question of local restrictions, a stretch beyond small-town decision-making toward a more national perspective. In any case, he would have to speak to Tim—maybe with Sheila present—about the general tone of public statements, the need to use language that carries you above any personal slight you may feel as a developer, however justified, to underline the positive, the progressive, the human side of the vision the family business is trying to promote.

So much for public relations. The more important problem was relations with the powers that be, now that the Environmental Commission was calling for a review of zoning regulations after this screwed-up Township Committee meeting where some local characters got up to offer their self-serving statements apparently without opposition from anybody supporting developers except the mayor. There was real danger if the people in Township Hall really got around to meddling with what the newspaper called "typical density regulations" used to determine "development parameters such as floor-to-area ratios" and how much of a lot is taken up by "impervious coverage." That kind of thing would be striking at the heart of Solar Estates' advanced vision for upgrading what the article itself called "these older neighborhoods." The right flexibility regarding floor-to-area ratios and maximum improvement coverage was crucial if Solar Estates hoped to build what it had to build in order to make a truly significant contribution to reshaping this sleepy, conservative, not to say reactionary town—even if it continued to vote Democrat.

Anyway, not to worry. Time now to head down to the Municipal Complex and check things out. Through the years he'd had very good relations with certain members of the administrative staff over there, and if the people he was seeing in the engineering section didn't respond the way he hoped, there were others he could turn to. He'd managed to keep up his tight connections to Princeton over a decade despite living elsewhere, but especially after Tim and Sheila finally agreed to set up an office here. Now that he thought about it, he wondered if that might not be part of the problem Solar Estates was having with these pin-headed critics, the fact that he himself wasn't really considered a local despite all the building he'd brought into the town. Maybe Tim was right about a lot of people being provincial in Princeton, snobbishly possessive or whatever you might call their superior attitude about where they happened to live.

Anyway, it was all just a technicality. He'd always worked with a local contractor over the years, shared the risk and the profit, and God knows spent time with those you had to know to do serious business in this town, not to mention playing the political game as was necessary. So as far as he was concerned, he was local enough to claim a close long-term relationship with the so-called Athens of America. And whenever necessary, he'd fed the hand that was most likely to feed him in the political arena, national, state, even local campaigns. This was something Tim and Sheila simply had to learn despite Tim's evident disillusionment with the way things worked sometimes in Washington to frustrate free enterprise. But Tim was still smarting over the problems of advancement he'd encountered in HUD due to internal politics during his stint down there. Not that Tim hadn't learned some things of professional value and made some useful contacts. It had still taken some doing to persuade him to give that scene up for the family enterprise and Dad had done his fair share of tutoring in the way of the world at the local level.

Tim's relative political innocence wasn't really a thing to worry about at this point. What mattered at the moment was how to convince the people in Township Hall not to go hog wild supporting new restrictions if this Environmental Commission got around to proposing radical changes, how to make a strong case for keeping the restrictions exactly where they were, at least as they applied to the plans already approved for the house on Independence Road and the one planned in Queenston

Park next to the Greek lady who was stirring things up. It was both a question of general policy and specific cases. Maybe the latter could serve the former. Maybe—no more time to think about it. He would just have to do the best he could, and God be with him.

There were only two people waiting in the conference room. One of them, maybe twice the age of the other, was more or less familiar from other encounters, though he wasn't the head man in the department. What was his name? Something Waterfield. The younger man, surely under thirty, was a complete stranger. He wondered if the recent local elections that had brought in the Democrats once again had anything to do with the changed personnel in this department. Or was the growing controversy and planned review keeping certain people in high places under cover while others were assigned to divert questions so long as the preliminary dirty work of investigation was in progress? Anyway, working with the second level wasn't likely to make his job any easier.

"I appreciate your following up on my phone call," Randy said. "To get right down to specifics, one of the plans I mentioned already has Township approval as you know, the one on Independence Road, so there's really no question about restrictions, new or old, in that case. The other plan I spoke about is still very much in the works. I've got an updated copy with me. Hardly final yet, but more to the point than the one you've seen."

"Yea," Waterfield said. "That's why the boss didn't think he needed to break another appointment to be here at this point, even informally, so to speak. He'll wait for your final plan, OK? But he sends his best."

"Well, I think we can get through this quickly. What I'd like to say for a start is that my more than ten years of experience in this territory tells me that the restrictions now in place are right for this region, as right as any in the state of New Jersey, and to change them now would create a hardship for both buyers and sellers."

"Well, that's certainly a point of view," Waterfield said. "And I'm sure both buyers and sellers will be taken into account. Already have been. A balanced perspective is what everyone in our business has in mind. But we aren't the ones to make the decision about new restrictions."

"Who makes the decision? I thought you were the ones who handle restrictions."

"Handle, yes," Waterfield said. "But enforcement is our responsibility, not legislation. That begins with the Planning Board."

"Right, I recognize there are studies and procedures. Levels you have to reach. But I'm sure you'll have a say in the matter. You're the people who know what's good for this town and what isn't."

"Most of the time. But it's a changing scene. Nature changes. People change."

"I don't worry about nature," Randy said. "I worry about what human beings do against their own best interests. Take the people who are so unhappy about our house over there on Independence Road. It's going to raise the property values like manna from heaven throughout that neighborhood. And the same goes for this lady who's so worried about her backyard view after I've built a two-million dollar gem next to her crummy cement-block ranch."

"Well, we'd like to have a word with you about that," Waterfield said.

"From what the lady had to say at the Township meeting, either she's reading plans we haven't seen or maybe she just doesn't understand the plans we have seen. But let's take a look at what you've got there."

"That's it. She doesn't understand. She thinks a construction rising ten feet from her border isn't legal."

"Well she's got a point. Should be fifteen feet at least. Let's have a look."

Randy spread the plans on the table. He ran his finger along the planned driveway that rose to a plateau in front of a three-car garage.

"This is what she's complaining about," Randy said. "Perfectly legitimate."

"Well, as I read it, the driveway is less than ten feet from the border, not fifteen," Waterfield said. "And in the view of the Queenston Park people, the house ought to be thirty feet from a neighbor's border. So the lady has a point."

"Yes, but it isn't the wall of the house itself we're talking about. That's here, thirty feet in from her border. As it's supposed to be."

The younger man stood up to have a look.

"So your position is that this rising construction at ten feet isn't part of the house?" Waterfield said.

"That's right. It's a driveway. With a retaining wall. A construction, not a building."

"Excuse me. I know the difference between a construction and a building."

Randy exhaled. "I'm sure you do. The point is, does this lady? Do the Queenston Park people? When it's a construction, the seven-foot restriction applies, not the thirty-foot restriction, and we're planning to expand from seven feet to at least ten feet. No small sacrifice."

Wakefield scratched his chest. "Sacrifice or not, the planning board will have to look into it now that a general question about the size and placing of these so-called McMansions has been raised by the Environmental Commission."

"Regarding the general question—I…"

"Excuse me, the point is, the issue's reached the Township Committee level already, and as elected officials they can't just let it float by. Get the message? Anyway, they have to look at both sides of the question, the owners you're involved with and the residents who are neighbors. Both are citizens, both are voters. I mean, they have to satisfy both somehow."

"I knew it," Randy said. "I knew it was a matter of politics."

"Well, you can call it that if you want, but I'd call it a matter of community responsibility."

"I won't argue language. Let me just say that I'd like you gentlemen to know I'm perfectly willing to play the political game. I've been around a long time, relatively speaking, and you can tell your boss that I know what's expected of me when it comes to politics. I'm fully prepared to make my contribution. Whatever the local party politics of the moment."

"You're getting way ahead of me," Wakefield said. "If that's the kind of politics you're taking about, you've got the wrong department. And if it's something else you're talking about, you'd better—"

"Don't get me wrong now. I'm talking strictly legal. Strictly open contribution."

"Anyway, I don't know why you're so worried. Once a restriction is in place, it usually stands in this town. Unless there are serious grounds for a revision."

"Well, I hope you don't think one lady's opinion is sufficient grounds."

"Depends on the lady," Waterfield said, smiling broadly, stepping back from the plans. "Only kidding. The fact is, there's more than one lady involved. And from what I hear, there may be more on the way."

Now that she thought about it, Cassie was sure she'd seen Amy Thornhill once or twice before their quick encounter in the corridor outside the Township Committee meeting, maybe just a nod from the other side of the road during her regular afternoon walk through the neighborhood, but her bright blond hair in braids bound tightly around her head and her very white skin were a certain sign that she had a northern European background of some kind that had stayed with her, though exactly what tobacco she smoked, as Father would put it, remained to be seen. Of course if you took that saying literally, you weren't likely to find many Queenston Park residents still smoking anything, most old enough to have given up tobacco several times, herself included, and no one she'd run into recently an obvious pot-smoking refugee from the Sixties. Anyway, she wouldn't be much good at recognizing that kind of past after having made her way through most of the Sixties on the other side of the Atlantic, where the forbidden thrills were different and where you had to be quite clever to get your share of them. Guitar-led rebellion, flower children, make love not war, little of that sort of thing in her white city, but you could sometimes find quick love in its byways, and the resistance songs of those nights during the junta years could break your heart.

Ah, enough of that. What chance was there of finding the revolutionary spirit alive in this upscale New Jersey neighborhood, with, as far as she could tell, mostly well-established professionals—doctors, lawyers, professors, engineers—decent solid citizens who'd probably smothered what rebellious impulses they may have had forty years ago, now settling quietly into the town's Democrat majority and mostly leaving debate and possible reform to the long roster of appointed boards and commissions and committees Nick had dug up for her from the internet: Flood and Stormwater Management Committee, Planning Board, Shade Tree Commission. Committees for Recreation, Affordable Housing, Sidewalk and Bikeway, Historic Preservation, Human Services, she couldn't remember half of them. And each of these, it seemed, would meet every now and then to review and maybe recommend this or that issue for further consideration by the five-member Township Committee that had the final authority to act or not act as it chose. At least so it seemed to her from that one lesson in local democracy she'd attended in person.

Exactly where Amy Thornhill stood on the housing issue she couldn't tell at that point. Her phone call to set up a meeting had been quick, rather breathy, as though she'd already started running off somewhere to stand her ground on something. And since she herself had agreed to the meeting right away, without discussion, really on impulse, she'd ended up with no clue from the lady's tone, no elaboration to work with, no room for anything more than a reference to environmental issues so general that it made you think she was afraid anything specific would suddenly wake up whatever authorities might be listening in on them. And of course the way things were these days, who could be absolutely sure you weren't being listened in on, especially if you traveled regularly out of the country and if you were a former European with a slight accent, which applied to both of them, though she'd call Amy's more Germanic than Mediterranean.

Paranoid? Maybe a bit. But as far as she was concerned, if you went back into fairly recent history with most Europeans, you were likely to find the kind of paranoia that came from memories of bad government. She'd seen enough of the early junta years to get a taste of that, enough of how the dictatorship could work on your psyche even if you were lucky enough to go abroad and remain on the periphery in the later years so you were spared what some of her friends had gone through during the student uprising at the Polytechnio. And now on this side of the Atlantic, where everybody but the poor Native Indians were once foreigners, what some still called the great melting pot no longer seemed as carefree about who belonged inside it and who didn't. She'd loved the feel of her America in the first years after she'd arrived, the sense that her life was her own to make what she could of it and that she would be protected from sudden intrusion, sudden political change, the neighborhood she'd chosen safe at any hour. The watching by others was for her benefit.

Why was that feeling of openness dying slowly for her? It wasn't only because of threats from outside. The land of the free—of course not counting Native Indians and slaves and that heritage—no longer seemed as protective of its freedoms at home, even if some of those in charge thought it their right and duty under God to bring their version of freedom to others by force. Ha. Bad government is a bad thing wherever, though maybe it was easier to escape the worry of it when you were very large rather than very small. Who could say? Anyway, from her point of view, America was still the best choice you could make, so enough of politics for an afternoon. Pooh.

As she crossed the bridge—the brook still full from the night's downpour—she stopped a minute to check out what looked like cement sandbags piled high against the near bank to protect the lawn rising sharply above it to the ranch house on the corner. Could the flood problem be that bad on this side of the Park? Only twice in the past thirty-odd years had she and Nick worried about flooding, both times after a hurricane had raised their section of the brook over the full spread of the back lawn, though not enough for the water to rise as high as the rear patio. Actually, for a while it had been fun to watch that water flow free beyond its banks, nature on a rampage for a few hours in this usually quiet green corner of the world, maybe not so quiet on this side of the Park. She turned the corner to face the front of Amy's house—nothing exceptional, a compact two-story cottage, newly painted, set back on a well-kept front lawn. Amy must have spotted her surveying the house, because she was standing in the open front door to greet her. At least her smile looked honest.

"I'm glad you've come," Amy said. "I worried that my call may have put you off. I seem to have become too careful about what I say over the phone."

"So have I," Cassie said. "Sometimes. At least when I call abroad."

"I'm sure I'm not important enough for anybody to listen in on me. It's just a feeling."

"Yes. I know the feeling."

Amy took her arm and led her into the living room—a European touch, Cassie thought. They sat at either end of a huge white sofa facing a bay window that offered a partial view of the brook's farther bank, thick with unattended growth.

"You're originally from Turkey," Amy said. "Somebody told me that."

"Greece," Cassie said. "Turkey once occupied our country, but they're just a neighbor now. Not always a friendly neighbor."

"Well, I'm originally from Austria, though I left very early. We too used to have trouble with neighbors. Often our fault. Anyway, the problems in this new country of ours once seemed on a much smaller scale. I'm not so sure anymore."

Cassie shifted into an easier angle on the couch and crossed her legs.

"I'm not so sure either. Anyway, you told me after the Township meeting the other day not to sell my house to Solar Estates. Is that what you want to see me about?"

"Yes. I can be more specific now. If you decide to sell your house, I hope you'll at least consider the possibility of selling it to the Township so that your lot can become open space."

"Selling it to the Township? How can we sell it to the Township?"

"Well, there's a fund. It's called a Land Trust. Anyway, it can help to finance that sort of thing. And I bet the Township has other sources, or can create them if there's enough pressure. The point is, those of us interested in keeping the brook from flooding our houses, especially in the area downstream from yours, would be grateful for any open space that can be created."

"I'm certainly in favor of open space," Cassie said. "The only problem is, I don't want to sell my house. And I certainly don't want to sell it to somebody who will tear it down. I want it to be lived in. I mean, I grew up believing in houses and I still believe in them."

"I understand," Amy said. "I believe in houses too. I—"

"Maybe you'll think me sentimental, but I believe houses have memories. They have ghosts. You can't just run away from them, abandon them like that overnight after living in them for thirty years."

"I understand. Believe me. My whole point is that I'm trying to save my own house and lot from further flood damage. At least keep my place in decent condition until I have to sell. I mean, both of us will have to sell at some point."

Cassie sighed. "I suppose. Unless my daughter in California wants the house. It just makes me uncomfortable to think about it at this point. Do I look that old?"

"Now I'm confused," Amy said. "From what you said at the Township meeting I thought you and your husband were actually considering an offer from one of these McMansion builders who've started coming into our neighborhood, and not always with much thought about what damage they may be causing. I'm sorry if I misunderstood."

"Well, this Solar Estates is talking about some kind of offer, but I'm not planning on going along with it. And my husband isn't either."

Amy's face relaxed. "Then I think we may still be on the same side. I won't bother you anymore about selling your house, but can I count on you to join those of us who are ready to fight for new restrictions that will prevent these megabuilders from taking over most of the neighborhood, chopping down trees and piling up huge mounds of earth so they can build towers and create a serious runoff problem to feed the serious flooding problem we already have?"

"Yes. Of course. Let me think. What would you want me to do?"

"Add your presence. Your voice. I don't know—your belief in houses. Like the house you live in."

"Well I'm not very good at making speeches. As I'm sure you saw at the Township meeting."

"That was a good speech. Came from the heart. Don't worry. When it comes to speeches, I learned enough about what is real and what isn't from my father's generation. You'll do fine. What I'm working on at the moment is a flood-control petition to take to the mayor's office, with the help of a Princeton senior who's an expert on local government. You can come in on that when it's ready. Gather names, etc. And join me at several Township meetings we ought to attend to get things moving in the right direction if we can. There's plenty to do. And I'd be grateful to have somebody near my age working along with me, OK?

Nick took a deep breath. It was a good time of year. The leaves on the trees were well along with their fall change but not yet floating down oppressively, and the air was just turning sharp enough in the late afternoon to let you know why the horizon ahead had a pre-winter clarity that honed the dying sun. Maybe later he'd take the canal path to Washington Road and back, get his fill of the early fall change and the crisp air, but now it was time to head over to Independence Road. He'd let Cassie and her new friend go on ahead to gather the few neighbors from their side of Queenston Park who'd agreed to show up for the exchange of ideas—is that really what Solar Estates had called it?—about the revised drainage plan for the latest McMansion rising in splendor above its neighbors on the far corner of the Park.

Cassie's new friend, Amy, had explained that the gathering wasn't really meant to be a protest, just a chance to find out what truths they could about this revised plan on the spot and ask some questions, especially embarrassing questions, and since Parker and his son were the ones who'd set up the meeting, as far as she was concerned not showing up would send the wrong message. That was so, she'd said, even if it just turned out to be a public relations move following up on the Parker son's apologetic letter in the local newspaper supposedly setting the record straight regarding his insulting interview several weeks back. She'd had great fun parodying that letter with flashes of ironic commentary, colored here and there by her remnant Germanic accent: the poor boy had used the wrong words (and he is a native speaker?), he'd simply meant to point out that a number of normal people in Princeton, as in the rest of America, were expressing a serious interest in larger homes, even luxury homes (more and more bedrooms and garages to dominate the neighbors, right?), and Solar Estates was merely trying to meet that need, thus enhancing rather than destroying relevant neighborhoods (more money for you and me and everybody, more water and waste in the sewers). And with open land in short supply, teardowns were simply bound to play a part in the town's expanding future (oh the pain, but oh the glory). Besides, he and his father had always been ready to consider reasonable requests from residents in the territory they were revitalizing, always ready to entertain new ideas for the improvement of the beautiful town of Princeton, New Jersey, etc. etc. (please, dear God, give us a break).

The lady had sure gotten into it, talking fast, making gestures, adding her choral comments with eyes toward heaven, and Cassie'd ended up nodding, then clapping her hands to show her delight. The trouble was, irony could take you only so far, because there were apparently enough people in town and out of town who wanted large homes—even large luxury homes—to keep these McMansion builders continually on the make, whatever the broader housing market. And there were apparently enough people willing to create space for them by selling their most substantial asset so they themselves could move into a larger home at one end of the scale or into a comfortable retirement facility at the other, a profitable deal either way. So—as the accommodating Mayor had asked—were the luxury buyers or eager sellers to be denied their right to have a future of their choice? And the hungry builders?

The simple answer was yes, they should be denied, or at least discouraged by better restrictions from going too far, too high, too indifferent to the surrounding environment. And some neighborhoods ought to be allowed to stay the way they'd grown naturally over the years, allowed to live in peace without becoming crowded, the houses as individual as they'd been shaped over the years and the lots as open to the sky, those living there free of fear that bulldozers might arrive to knock down trees and make fodder of the teardown next door, then hover there overnight as though waiting to eat you next. Yes, you had to challenge constriction, fight for what open space was left, keep the way clear for the sun. And he was ready to say that in public when he could do so without upstaging Cassie.

The one thing he didn't want to do was complicate her new passion for local political action—if passion was the right word. Since they'd settled in the States she'd never had more than a general interest in politics, though certainly enough to keep up her side of a conversation about what was going on in Washington or somewhere in Europe that roused her special interest—but no particular heat. That is, unless it was some rare bit of news from the home country that touched a nerve, such as the Cyprus issue, which could make her abruptly an outspoken Greek partisan of the dispossessed. Or the plight of refugees in the Middle East or Africa, which could lead to a bit of old-country swearing about the callousness of those who were choosing to face the other way. Now that he thought about it, maybe that strong sympathy for the dispossessed came from the same source as her firm sense of place, of home, what she'd once called the only semblance of permanence there was, a thing that only a house you'd lived in for years could really bring you.

But how do you take this sense forward so it works for you at the level of political action in the Township of Princeton, NJ? After that meeting of the Township Committee he'd begun to feel just as boxed in as Cassie said she'd felt, though he'd thought it best not to tell her so at that moment—just as uncertain about what anybody out of power could do to challenge a system that seemed to prevent any possibility of change, any appeal by ordinary citizens for at least a serious review of inadequate restrictions. Sure, you could talk at a meeting of this or that committee of volunteers or even paid members responsible for reviewing this or that aspect of public planning, but where was that talk likely to go? And if your issue actually found its way onto an agenda before the elected Township Committee, what was further talk likely to produce when there was so much commercial and political influence stacked against the private citizen?

Still, he wasn't about to discourage Amy's attempt to work for change within the system, her focus on attending public meetings of the Environmental Commission and the Flood and Stormwater Management Committee and the Planning Board, pressing anyone she could to help her try to persuade committee members to see that most new McMansions were not only out of proportion to their neighbors but—as she argued—a challenge to the environment. Especially through the way they swallowed permeable ground and contributed to the problem of water disposal and erosion along the brooks, including Harry's Brook at the foot of her lawn. But she was well ahead of her neighbors in fighting for new regulations that way, and even farther ahead when she talked about the need to move on up from local agencies to engage county and state officials, her voice sometimes taking on the tone of someone running for office.

Which was all right for her, why not? She seemed to know a great deal about the ins and outs of local politics, even to the point of hinting that there could have been some hanky-panky going on with certain of the McMansion operations, quid pro quos of one kind or another. God knows the town needed knowledgeable people like her, committed citizens offering honest public service, not only those on committees but private citizens ready to speak out when the occasion arrived. But given Cassie's usual low key approach to things, he wasn't sure how she could fit into that mode comfortably, and if she did, if she went into the sort of campaign mode Amy had in mind, what role could he play to help?

He turned the corner onto Independence Road and paused to have a good look at the Solar Estates McMansion still in the last stage of progress a block away where the road swerved sharply north, to see if it was as ugly at this distance as Cassie had reported. He decided it wasn't ugly, it was grotesque, three houses glued into one, a huge center and two appendages rising as though on a steep hill, the spread of it serving the full vista at that end of the street, partial veneer of stone for the central facade, clapboard elsewhere, the whole three stories high with a black shingle roof, one appendage below serving as a stumpy two-story bridge to nowhere, the other—linked to the center by a shorter bridge of ceiling-high windows—a two-story three-car garage tall and long enough for indoor basketball and set at an angle as if a miscalculated after-thought. Huge boulders cut through the lot on one side to protect the ascending path to the garage from the low-lying rest of the lot and, on the other side, to create a wall against the 50-year old ranch-house development beyond.

He walked a while to check that out. As far as he could tell, no single one of the thirty-odd houses was exactly the same as its neighbor, the various roofs and additions, even the carports, seemingly part of an imaginative act by its owner to be individual—and this the territory where a group of owners was said to be petitioning for the whole to become a historical site. Nick shook his head: and next door, the mega king of the mountain, an eyeless Cyclops monster with a broken arm, trying to hold sway over his more creative, rebellious serfs.

He crossed over and headed up the street toward the group gathered in a rough circle at the foot of the McMansion lot, some eight or nine people, mostly women, who he assumed were local residents, Cassie and Amy at the far end, Tim Parker facing the center, holding a rolled-up plan that he was using to emphasize a point. He was in work mode—black jacket, dirty jeans, heavy boots—and he stood there stiffly with legs apart, in that posture stockier than his father, tanned, his thick neck suggesting that he might have been a football lineman in college. Nick moved in next to Cassie and put his arm around her waist, then took it away. Cassie smiled at him, then linked her arm in his.

"As I've already tried to affirm," Tim was saying, "this is my project, in fact my house, mine and Sheila's, not my father's, so you can consider me the one qualified to answer any questions. He's not here by choice, because he wants me to assume the responsibility, and that's all right by me. Sheila's here to make sure I stay on the straight and narrow, right Sheila?"

Nick spotted Sheila nodding a certain shy assent at the opposite end of the group. Amy looked up from the pad she was holding.

"So who was responsible for the decision to build this house so large and so high above the neighboring properties?" Amy asked. "If that was your decision, it was a dangerous one in view of the drainage problem in this area."

"We're fully aware of that problem," Tim said. "It was exactly because of the water table conditions here that I was forced to raise the house three feet."

"Three feet?" somebody said. "Who are you kidding? It looks like twenty feet to me."

"Depends on where you're looking from," Tim said. "Where you're counting from. We count from the original base, not the road where you're standing."

"Well, wherever you count from, the runoff is going to be a problem," Amy said. "However high the house, the ground in this neighborhood is mostly clay and doesn't absorb very well. And your house has taken up much of what land there was to absorb the runoff."

Tim sighed. "Can't win, can I? Water runs off. It has to go somewhere. And everything we've done is within the regulations. Ask the Engineering Department. Ask the Zoning Board. Try to be a little patient."

"We're trying," a white-haired lady down the line said. "We only have so much time to be patient. One more good flood and we're moving out I don't know where to."

"There won't be any flooding," Tim said. "You forget what I showed you on the plans. We've sunk two huge tanks in the front area to catch most of the runoff."

"And where does the water go from the tanks?" Amy said. "Right back into the system that carries it down to Harry's Brook. Just adding that much more to the overflow problem."

"Well, where did the water go before?" Tim asked. "You can't stop the rain from coming down, for Christ's sake."

"Much of it went into the ground," Amy said. "As best it could. But you've killed that by building such a huge house over so much of the permeable land. So as far as I'm concerned, tanks or whatever won't really help much."

"We're just doing our best to solve a general problem," Tim said. "If you had your way, nobody would ever be able to build anything in this part of town."

"That's not so," a gray-haired man wearing a baseball cap said.

"There's never been an empty lot around here. And when there is one, people build something within reason."

"I give up," Tim said. "There's never an empty lot here yet people build on empty lots here within reason. Talk about having it both ways."

Cassie unlinked her arm from Nick's and took a half step forward.

"Shame on you. How can you talk like that to a man so much older than you? And shame on you for doing what you're doing to our neighborhood, whatever regulations you've found a way to use. Just look at this, this, monstrosity you've created. I say shame, shame, shame."

Nick gazed at her. He felt like clapping. He looked down the row: two in the line had their heads bowed, the others were watching Tim, who had slapped the roll in his hand. Sheila stood there with her chin thrust out.

"OK, I've had it," Tim said. "Thanks for coming by. Send me an e-mail if you have any further questions. God bless."

He turned and climbed up toward the garage, swinging his rolled plans this way and that like a tennis racket. Sheila followed him a pace behind.

CHAPTER Four

Randy arrived a few minutes early at Lahiere's, and though he didn't want to show himself as too eager, too concerned, by being exactly on time for what was likely to be an awkward lunch any way you sliced it, he counted on Nick Mandeville coming in a bit late in keeping with what seemed to be chic thing to do in that town. This meant he ought to have time for a quick scotch on the rocks, so he headed down the steps into the bar on the left. It was empty. He decided it wasn't his favorite kind of bar even if it had been his choice: a touch too formal, with a print at the far end by that short-legged French cartoonist—a woman from another age gazing down through binoculars from a balcony—and next to that, an old poster ad for Vermouth Bianco Martini Rossi. But on the back wall behind the stool he settled on, above the spread of tables, there were some nice outdoor country paintings of animals in woodland and horses grazing contentedly, all of that creating a friendlier atmosphere to help his mood.

Not that he was really worried about having to deal with the situation the Mandeville woman was creating along with that other European woman—after all, he had the high cards, enough of the right connections—but a little preliminary scotch wouldn't do any harm in calming his nerves. The problem was, these people over at the Municipal Building had one eye on reality and another eye on politics. The reality was, you couldn't stop progress. Cut the legs out from under Solar Estates and you could bet your life somebody else would come along to fill the gap overnight, somebody with less interest in talking to anybody about anything. The Princeton scene was just too valuable, quality property still much in demand, the profit margin always good enough whatever might be happening elsewhere in the state and beyond. But politics threw a wrench into things. You had a bunch of liberals—lawyers, doctors, professors, whatever—all out there trying to keep things just the way they were, mostly middle-class types or worse but completely conservative when it came to moving ahead, when it came to using the free enterprise system for their own good. And once they started agitating, the wives especially, going to meetings and raising this issue or that, the Municipal Building had to pretend, at least, that it was all ears.

He'd tried to counter this new challenge, put a lid on it, by sending Tim out to meet some of these so-called protesters over on Independence Road, but that seemed to have made things worse, fired up a couple of the ladies, this Mandeville lady and her friend in particular. So the first chance they got, they went for the Zoning Board of Adjustment and the Environmental Commission, who knows where else, raised some kind of hell over there, got them to promise they'd look again into the restrictions on height and drainage and the rest that they'd already looked into once and found too complicated for immediate action, no surprise. And that had just made Tim get hot under the collar. Maybe sending the boy out on that mission to answer questions had been a mistake. He'd apparently lost his cool and cut the thing short when he saw the mood getting unfriendly, ended up taking it out on Sheila for suggesting he might try to be a little more diplomatic. Told her to fuck diplomacy, you either believe in a project or you don't, either believe in him or you don't, ended up bringing her to tears. He must have felt humiliated or something. Their problems were their problems, but he couldn't really blame the kid for getting aggravated at all the criticism going on around him, even if he did get discouraged too easily sometimes. Anyway, that sort of confrontation with the neighborhood couldn't really affect the house on Independence Road. That house was water over the dam.

What he had to worry about now was the lot next to the Mandevilles— not worry, really, he'd gotten what seemed to him a pretty good hearing over at the Municipal Building on the latest set of plans for that project without having to spell out too openly how much he was willing to help those who helped him when it came to the next election cycle, but once people started showing up at meetings and sounding off, you could never be certain how deep the favorable climate was and how long it would hold. One thing you could be certain of was that nothing was likely to be a problem in the short run because nothing really threatening over there at the Municipal Building happened in the short run. Time was on your side, a lot of time. But still, Solar Estates had to keep going at its own speed while there was momentum, while both generations of the family still had their full hearts in the business.

"Yeah, let me have another. Light on the rocks, right?"

The thing at hand might be settled best if he could get Nick Mandeville to put a leash on his bride and go along with what was clearly the best deal for their future. The man had struck him as more reasonable than his wife, slower to rush to judgments, willing to hear you out at least. He hadn't known what to expect when he finally got through to the professor at his college number, but the low-key approach, just a calm request to have a chance to clarify the latest plans relating to the house next to Dr. Mandeville's, worked in the end, even if he was told that he could drop the "Dr." Not exactly rude, but not exactly friendly either. Anyway, the man finally agreed to meet him, so who gave a fuck what he wanted to be called—just plain old professor or plain old Nick or plain old kiss my ass, whatever. There he was.

"Have a seat, Doc. I mean Prof. Glad to see you. Can I order you something?"

"Maybe I'll have a glass of wine with lunch," Nick said. "But go ahead, finish your drink."

"That's all right. I'll take it with me. Let's move over to a table. You don't mind eating in the bar area, do you? Sort of cozier in here."

"Fine by me. I'm on a rather tight schedule, so I—"

"I mean I really appreciate you're taking the time for us to get together. Seriously. I know how busy you are. I wouldn't have bothered you if the situation—if there wasn't something I think is important. For both of us."

"You've got new plans for the house next to mine, is that it? You said something about new plans over the phone."

"Well that's part of it. But before I get to that, let me be completely open with you. I mean put all my cards on the table. As you know, some of the people in your neighborhood have been raising hell in the press and over at the Municipal Building about the house on Independence Road. Which is their right. Your lady and her friends included."

"Well I wouldn't really call it raising hell. I'd call it asking important questions about—"

"Don't misunderstand me. I'm all in favor of people asking questions and exchanging ideas and attending meetings. That's democracy. And I think my son Tim—you may have seen his published apology—probably went too far in what he said about Princeton residents in that earlier interview. But the problem is the future. If the Township starts playing around with the zoning restrictions, I mean the people in charge over there, God knows where that could end up in terms of killing progress in this town."

"Well, that depends on what you mean by progress," Nick said.

"Of course. I understand that. To put it in personal terms, I'm talking about the kind that interests you and me. I mean your need at some point soon to move out of where you are and get on with your life comfortably as a senior citizen, and my need to see that I can pass on a healthy business to my son and his bride. We're talking about family values, something that both of us believe in. Which is what convinces me that you and I may be able to work things out as partners."

"Partners?"

"In a manner of speaking," Randy said, leaning forward. "What I have in mind is, you know, sharing in whatever profit there would be in building under the present restrictions on both your property and the one next door. Everything strictly legal, strictly environmental, in keeping with the current regulations."

"The only problem is, the current regulations aren't good enough," Nick said.

"They've been good enough for some years now and they're bound to stay that way for some years ahead. That's the reality. So long as things don't get stirred up again politically. And in that connection, I'm willing to up the option ante on your house so that we end up on the same page."

"But I'm not selling my house. My wife, Cassie, won't hear of it. I won't hear of it. I haven't retired yet, and even when I do..."

"I understand your situation. Honestly. My family means every-thing to me. We may have our agreements and our disagreements, our worries etcetera, but family comes first. You and your wife have got your future to worry about, my future is in passing things on to my son and daughter-in-law. So we should be able to do business together."

"How's that exactly?"

"If you really don't want to sell your house, can I make it worth your while one way or another to stay out of my way regarding the house I'm going to build next door to yours?"

"Worth my while? You're talking about a payment of some kind?"

"Not at all. Relax. I'm talking about giving you the right to approve the final plans for that house next door. I'll honor what objections you have and your wife's as well. Within reason, of course. And I'll up the option ante on your house well above its current market value just in case you change your mind."

"In return for?"

"For getting your wife and her friends to cool it. I mean getting them to let things go ahead as they're going to go anyway. That's all. Think about it."

The waiter stood there holding the menus, then delicately handed them out. He took a step back and stood there waiting. "Drinks to start?" he asked finally.

"I'll have a glass of chardonnay," Nick said. "And Oysters Mignonette for an appetizer. Then I think I'll go for the Honey-Roasted Duck Crepe with Fontina."

Randy was still studying the menu. "Christ Almighty," he said. "Don't they have a straight American dish for lunch in this place? You've got to be an expert in foreign languages to know what the fuck you're ordering half the time."

Cassie was disappointed by the turnout for the open meeting of the Flood and Stormwater Management Committee. The previous morning she'd covered as much neighboring territory as she comfortably could with the phone numbers she'd been given, even planted a few handwritten notices in Queenston Park mailboxes, and though surely not equal to what Amy had tried to cover, it was as much as she felt she could usefully do in a neighborhood where she really knew few people by name. She decided the Harry's Brook flood problem was not an issue that moved many hearts beyond those of the old-timers who actually bordered on the brook, and most of those old-timers apparently did not move easily outside their daily routines. There weren't more than five or six people in the conference room sitting outside the table reserved for Committee members, and some of those must have been local reporters, notepads at the ready. When she complained about the numbers to Amy, her friend showed a kind of "what else is new" face and whispered that this meant the two of them would just have to speak up that much more firmly and loudly—not the kind of advice to put her at ease.

The group at the Committee table struck her as a curious mixture: the chairman a heavy man with a fringe of white hair and a very sober expression, one elderly woman with glasses hanging around her neck, beside her a man who looked young enough to be a graduate student, then a well-groomed woman in her late thirties and a man with a beard just beginning to show some gray. The chairman had called the roll and was now moving toward the screen beyond the far end of the table. The lights went down and an aerial photograph appeared on the screen, a stretch of land and houses adjacent to what looked to her like several streams joining at one point. Nothing there seemed familiar.

"Queenston Park," Amy whispered. "Part of it."

The chairman stood beside the screen holding a flashlight pointer. The audience came to life for a moment.

"I think he taught geology somewhere," Amy leaned over to say. "He's supposed to know a lot about erosion and rocks."

The chairman was talking to the screen about streambeds. He was saying that streambeds were a thing you couldn't really understand from a photograph. To simplify matters, he wanted to explain that streambeds in this area normally had an ancient history going back to the Ice Age, northern New Jersey was all ice once, and streambeds were mostly hard as cement by now, impermeable, which meant you couldn't do all that much about streambeds at this point. Streams meandered, he said, eating away one bank only to balance the loss by adding to the opposite bank. Trees were uprooted by erosion but could sprout again elsewhere.

The chairman paused, faced his audience. The problem in any case, he said, was water flow, which was variable, decreased at times of drought, increased at times of heavy rain, not by raindrops so much as runoff, though, the truth be told, runoff from impervious surfaces caused by new construction was not really a major issue.

Pause again. Back to the screen. It was nature that caused erosion, he said emphatically. Excessive water from rain caused erosion. And floods had cycles of severity, two years, five years, ten years, a hundred years. No way to avoid floods. No way to avoid periods of drought or heavy rain. And bridges could prove to be obstructions, causing backup, causing further awkward meandering for streams through the flood plain.

The chairman circled a bridge with his pointer and traced a section of stream. Any questions so far?

Amy raised her hand. "You seem to be saying that all the erosion caused by Harry's Brook on our properties is nobody's fault, just a natural development we can't do anything about."

"I'm not saying that exactly," the chairman said. "What I'm saying is that flooding and erosion can be complicated issues and in any case have a historical basis and a basis in nature."

"But what are we property owners supposed to do about the damage the brook is doing? Just sit there and hope nature behaves better?"

"Well, nature behaving better would certainly help," the chairman said with a little chuckle. "Periods of heavy rain and hurricanes certainly don't help."

Amy nudged Cassie. Cassie raised her hand and received a nod.

"But how does this Committee expect us to stop heavy rains and hurricanes?" Cassie said. "Make sacrifices to the gods?"

The chairman lowered his pointer. "Well, the Committee can't stop heavy rains and hurricanes either. The point is, I'm just hoping for a reasonable, factual, non-hysterical discussion of the subject based on natural history."

"You think we're being hysterical?" Cassie asked. "You've seen the condition of the land along the brook. You've walked through our back yards and seen the erosion and the lack of drainage and the falling trees. You don't need an aerial map to tell you how bad things are at ground level."

The chairman sighed. He turned back toward his seat.

"I'm just trying to keep things in proper perspective," he said, his voice tired. "Maybe it would help for us to hear from our Township consultant at this point. Maybe his expertise will convince you of what I apparently can't. Let me introduce you to Ralph Merriweather, head of the New Brunswick-based Stormwater Consulting Agency. Mr. Merriweather."

The man with a beard nodded right and left. "My pleasure to be here. Let me dive right into the subject of our meeting, Harry's Brook.

It is indeed complicated, as the Chair suggests. For a start, I can't say that new development in recent years taking place in the relevant neighborhoods connects the flooding we have in mind with an increase in impervious surface. For flooding, there seems to be a twenty to thirty year cycle, even if nobody can prove it. Because of the random nature of floods, you can't tie their origin to any single cause. Is that clear enough?"

The lady with the dangling glasses sat back. "Are you saying that land development has no effect on reducing impervious surface?"

"There is development and there is development. Single house development has little effect, though it may contribute to a runoff problem. But my point is, most things are random. Nature is random. It could rain for three years or you could have a three-year drought."

"So nobody's to blame for what nature does, is that it?"

"Many things in life are random. Stuff happens, as they say. Origins of flooding are difficult to determine and so is blame."

The well-groomed woman raised her hand. "Well, one origin of flooding is too much water in brooks and streams. We're trying to determine what causes that, aren't we?"

"Of course. I'm just trying to share with you the facts of life. Flood plains are natural occurrences. The channel of Harry's Brook was not formed by a shovel or a bulldozer, it was formed by erosion. The wear and tear on a flood plain is like that on a heavily used carpet, and you can't stop walking on a carpet."

"Huh?"

"Excuse me," Amy said. "Did you say carpet?"

"Right."

Amy stood up. "This is ridiculous. How can you compare our damaged backyards to an overused carpet?"

The chairman stood up. "Please. Please sit down. I insist on order."

Amy sat down. Silence.

The woman with the dangling glasses leaned forward again. "I must say that all this talk about nature and erosion and carpets and nobody being to blame makes me wonder why this Committee is necessary at all. Since apparently nothing can be done about anything and nobody is accountable, how are we supposed to assess the damage that is being done and what we can do about it?"

"That's a good question," Mr. Merriweather said. "Unfortunately, I'm not in a position to answer that. It goes way beyond my charge as consultant."

Somebody in the audience apparently representing the engineering department suggested that the first thing needed was measurements to determine exactly what the erosion along Harry's Brook had caused in terms of land loss, tree loss, permeable space loss, etc. That might be a starting point.

Cassie stood up. "It seems nobody wants to blame anybody for anything. So let's not blame anybody, especially not developers who build huge houses for the comfort of those who need great comfort and three garages for their cars. When the floods come, let's just line up on our lawns and pour libations to the gods. That may not be democracy, but at least it means this Committee doesn't have to take any action and it means nobody has to be blamed."

The chairman turned to her. "Frankly, I don't think that's being fair."

"Of course it isn't being fair," Cassie said. "To be fair you would have to blame somebody for not having dealt with the disaster we face and not dealing with it now, and continue to hope this might lead to some action. Preferably by this Committee, which is supposed to represent us ignorant citizens in coping with the flooding problem in our once very green town."

"I think the speaker has a point," the young man just out of graduate school said. "This Committee should look into the matter, and beyond that, the parameters of our charge."

"Certainly," the chairman said. "We will look into the matter in due course. But in a spirit of fairness to the various sides of the issue."

"What sides?" Cassie said. "I mean how…"

"Will you please sit down," the chairman said. "Your idea of democracy seems to be that you can speak whenever you want for as long as you want. That isn't the way we operate in this country."

Amy stood up. "Is that right?" she said. "Tell us how we operate in this country. By allowing you to decide …"

"Enough," the chairman said. "In the name of decency, enough."

Was he hearing noises, footsteps, across the way or just the shades of his obsession wandering through his brain? Nick put his book down and crossed to the row of windows in the living room that looked out on the house next door. No movement, total silence. He turned back. If he was losing his cool, he could see why Cassie and Amy had returned quietly furious from their the second meeting with Tim Parker on Independence Road, a meeting initiated by him but apparently tense from the start and ending as abruptly as the first, no sign of a change in attitude on the part of Solar Estates, no hope for reasonable dialogue, at least not as far as the younger generation was concerned. Still, it might have helped prepare her for that meeting if he'd remembered to give her a few more details about his lunch with Tim Parker's old man, not only his irony about Randy's offer of a partnership and his final impression that the man was really just an operator who claimed to put all his cards on the table while keeping a few jokers in his pocket, but his sense that son Tim was the real problem in the family.

That had come late in the lunch when Randy had tried to work in a bit of unwelcome intimacy by saying that he had to admit Tim and Sheila were struggling with a few personal problems still unclear to him, difficult to talk about, but obviously creating moments of strain between them so that both of them were on edge a times and not always in command of their best selves. He'd said maybe it had to do with the delay in her getting pregnant, maybe it had to do with her occasionally feeling left out in what was supposed to be a fully shared business. You know about families, he'd said, leaning back in his chair: the only worthwhile life there is, but what keeps a marriage ticking, what keeps people from tearing each other apart sometimes, God only knows. Then he'd smiled a kind of dip-headed Ronald Reagan aw-shucks smile.

After hearing Cassie's account of what had happened on Independence Road, he wasn't sure that kind of inside information from Dad would have made any difference. Though Tim had been the one to invite the so-called Amy Thornhill Group to that meeting, there was no sign that he understood what he was facing, what he was up against, no sign that Amy and Cassie and their friends had any intention of pulling back in what they now called their campaign. Apparently Tim had more or less stonewalled. The presence of some fifteen or twenty irate local residents, at least double the number that had gone out there the first time, evidently failed to intimidate him in the slightest. Cassie described him standing on the front lawn in his work clothes, arms crossed in front of him, leaning against one of the few remaining trees near the front boundary line, this one bearing a "No Trespassing" sign that had gone up since his earlier public interview there. Cassie reported that they'd been careful not to trespass, which had made talking to the man difficult because they had to shout over a strip of new sod he'd just brought in, presumably too precious for him to cross so they could be face to face.

According to her account, dialogue proved to be largely irrelevant anyway. When they'd brought up the issue of exactly what his building was still adding to the flood problem through runoff water, he'd apparently pointed out the two newly buried containers that were supposed to take care of that on one front, and the great boulders he'd brought in to create some kind of barrier on another front, and then he'd asked people to relax, the amount of runoff water that might be added to the pot from his house was not going to flood anybody's basement near or far. Several people insisted that their basements had already been flooded, they'd had to pump out the water, do major clean-up. Tim, it seems, just shook his head: couldn't be true, but if true, that would be taken care of by the sunken containers in due course. And the impermeable surface his vast footprint had created? Not a problem, just wait and see.

This had apparently brought Amy into the dialogue: what about the question of comparative size, the huge dimensions of his mansion in relation to its much smaller neighbors? Look around, Tim had said, spreading his arms like a holy man: many shapes, things are born, grow, find their right proportions from generation to generation, that's life, and you can't stop life in a free enterprise society. Cassie reported that when she'd finally had the audacity to ask him if he was at least going to bring in an architect to help him make a more reasonable design for the mansion he planned to build next to her house, he'd thrown up his hands and said something like "OK, I've had enough. You people aren't interested in having a serious exchange of ideas, so I bid you good day, good night, God be with you now and forever more," then turned and marched off to disappear inside his three-car garage.

That had killed the encounter but had also fired up the campaign against those—meaning not only Solar Estates—who were creating what the protesting group called "an environmental disaster" in the local press report. Nick didn't yet know exactly what next steps were being debated at Amy's place where the leaders of her group, now including Cassie, were gathered to work that out, but the report said a number of residents in the area were planning some sort of joint appeal to the Township Committee, Amy's group joined by another group so that it could mean forty to fifty people facing the Township Committee. The other group was protesting against the environmental consequences of some project that would fill two heavily wooded hillside lots on one edge of town with a building complex meant to house at least eighty so-called senior citizens fifty-five years of age and older. Nick had read that one aspect of the problem was the limited senior citizen housing available in the township, a growing need among long-standing residents that Township Hall felt hadn't yet been sufficiently addressed, though the developer's insistence on a lower limit of fifty-five struck Nick as a way of soliciting those buyers with an assured income and years ahead to enjoy the fruits of their pensions or shrewd investments or whatever.

Forty to fifty people arriving in that Township Hall theater to state their case? That would surely be a first. And those five solemn faces on the raised platform would surely listen patiently when the time arrived for audience participation, and the recording secretary would take it all down if people spoke up loudly enough. But then what? Surely there would be lawyers there to represent the developers, challenge those un-initiated in debate, win enough points for one or another of those five heads to shake in agreement with this or that point, maybe even grant a good point from the floor with a nod of the head, speaking out only for clarification before each returned to a silent, immobile, mask-like sobriety. Time would be called in due course, there would be no vote because there would be nothing official to vote on, no recommendation would become a firm route to action because recommendations were only suggestions in that context, debate would move to the corridor outside but no doubt only briefly before people drifted off to a late dinner. Nick again began to feel the frustration, the sense of being trapped by a system that didn't really give you a chance, didn't really represent you, and was too bureaucratic to allow him or Cassie or even Amy to find a way to—

No mistake now: footsteps outside the front door and then the doorbell, loud, twice. He turned on the outside light. The man he found standing two paces back from the screen door was not in uniform, so it couldn't be UPS or Federal Express. He was tall, dark-haired, trimmed moustache, unsmiling, you might call him good-looking if he weren't already lined for somebody forty-ish, and heavy in the waist. His eyes looked at him steadily.

"What can I do for you?" Nick said.

"Detective Mark Masseli. My badge. I'd like to have a word with the lady of the house, if I may. Mrs. C. Mandeville?"

"Right. Step in. She's not at home at the moment. Why do you want to see her?"

The detective stepped into the front hallway. "A bit of official business. When do you expect her back?"

"Not long. She's at a meeting."

"What kind of meeting might that be? If I'm not intruding to ask."

"Come on in and let me close the door. It's getting chilly out there. A political meeting. Well, not exactly. An environmental meeting."

Detective Masseli took out a small black notebook, opened it to have a look, then put it away.

"Environmental, you said? Would that be something to do with Solar Estates?"

"For a start," Nick said. "But others too. What's the problem?"

"Well, let me just say we'd like to have a word with the lady as soon as possible."

"Who's 'we'?"

"We? 'We's' the Township Police Department. At this point it's— well, it's me."

"Can you tell me what it's about?" Nick asked. "I mean I'd like to know what it's about before I go looking for my wife and get her involved."

"She's already involved or I wouldn't be here," Detective Masseli said, shifting his feet.

"But in what? What's happened?"

"Well, I think I can say what's happened so far is the disappearance of the guy who runs Solar Estates. The young guy, not the old guy. Which, in a word, is why I'd like to talk to your wife."

"Disappearance? What does that mean?"

"That's what we're trying to find out. What I'm trying to find out."

"And you think my wife's somehow involved?"

Detective Masseli shifted his feet again. "I don't think I'm at liberty to say any more at this point in time. But let me say that somebody has reported that there was a threat against this Timothy Parker over there on Independence Road during some kind of protest. I mean that your wife said something threatening, and I'm afraid we have to take that seriously at this point in our investigation when a disappearance is involved."

"My wife said something threatening? Like what?"

"All I can tell you at this point is that it was reported as a threat with a gun. Sorry, but I have to leave it there for the time being."

"And I'm sorry, but the idea of a threat of that kind or any other kind is ridiculous."

"Maybe so, maybe not, my friend. Anyway, I won't take your time any longer. I'd like you to call the Township Police Department when the Missus gets home and then I'll return to have a word with her."

"Well I'll go get her now. She's in the neighborhood."

"No, you just let her come home naturally. I don't want her or anybody else to be alarmed at this point in time. The investigation is just beginning."

Cassie thought Nick's voice had sounded odd over the phone, not quite normal, sort of hesitant, as though he felt somebody was listening in on the line: "Come home as soon as you comfortably can, OK? Tell our friends over there, well, tell them I don't know what, that I've picked up a virus or something, whatever excuse is easy for you. I'll explain when you get here." And then he'd added, clearly not just an afterthought: "Don't hurry when you get outside, just look your natural self, I mean unconcerned, whatever, just in case somebody's watching."

Sure. No problem, as they say these days. Except somebody like who? Look natural? Of course. She didn't want the person or persons watching her to get the idea that a message like that might make her nervous walking home in the dusk. And of course she should have no trouble finding an excuse to leave the meeting and go home suddenly that way, just say, "my husband thinks somebody is watching me for some reason he won't reveal and wants me home as soon as possible because he's gone out of his mind." Well, she didn't know if it was the unconcerned thing to do, leaving her quick departure up to Amy, taking Amy aside to say there was trouble at home, you can tell them my husband's sick or something, and I'll call you tomorrow. Amy had studied her a moment, then nodded. At least she didn't say, "No Problem."

Now that Cassie was out in the cool air, the sun down but still some pleasing afterglow through the trees up ahead, the walk home felt safe enough, even refreshing—that is, once the image, the fear that was suddenly making her shiver, went away. It hadn't come back for years now, not since she'd really settled in Princeton. There was no concierge around to trigger it the way that bald character in their Athens apartment building did more than once during the first year of their marriage, when Nick decided to spend the remnant of his sabbatical in Greece during the last months of the Junta. The concierge was a filthy man with a fake smile she'd never liked but got to hate when she learned that various such live-in doormen and sometimes their wives were not just the usual front-door gossips here and there along the street but domestic spies working hand in hand with the dictatorship, maybe reporting on who was saying what about the current situation but certainly who of possible interest was visiting whom. And finally in the case of their hairless monster, leading two of the Junta thugs to the girl's apartment below theirs and causing that young thing with the wild hair and long eyelashes to disappear completely after she returned to find her apartment in shambles and most of the manuscript she was writing torn to shreds. Talk about getting nervous being watched.

After that she could barely bring herself to walk past the concierge's desk in the foyer, let alone wish him good day. And once in the street she sometimes couldn't get rid of the feeling that a planted Junta thug was just waiting to jump out from behind a dusty pepper tree or a basement love-nest to arrest her for the company they were keeping in those days and the subversive ideas in her head. Given the company, mostly restless artists and intellectuals who had chosen not to go off to Paris, some involved, she was certain, in who knows what version of more or less passive resistance to the Colonels, the only thing she felt might keep her safe was Nick's American citizenship. For a while she simply didn't go out unless Nick was with her, his passport in his pocket, but that ended up impossibly confining. It was the city she'd learned to love in her school days and she wasn't about to let anything frighten her into staying inside. Anyway, whatever the recent developments in her adopted land of the free and the brave, there was really no excuse now for the chill that had come over her again, no need to talk up her courage to herself by—well, surprise surprise...

"I didn't mean for you to walk all the way home by yourself," Nick said. "But you headed out from Amy's so quickly, I couldn't meet up with you sooner. Are you all right? You look pale."

"I'm all right. Considering I'm supposed to walk unconcerned even though unnamed people may be watching my every move."

"I'm sorry I had to say that. I guess I'm getting paranoid, but I wasn't certain any longer that our phone wasn't tapped, so for the record I just repeated what the detective said to me. I suppose it's ridiculous to worry about phone tapping in Princeton, except for the fact that we happen to go out of the country often. Used to, anyway."

"What detective?"

"Sorry. I'm out of breath. The detective who came to interview you. He told me not to say anything that would send out an alarm. Again, ridiculous. Alarm to whom? Where? In our neighborhood?"

Nick was trying to smile now. Cassie took his arm.

"Everything's ridiculous. Fine. Of course. But in the name of the Holy Virgin, what is all this you're talking about?"

"It's complicated. For a start, apparently Randy Parker's son, Tim, has disappeared."

"Disappeared? What does that mean?"

"I don't really know what it means. The man wouldn't give me any details. All I know is that Tim Parker has disappeared and this detective was told that you had threatened him."

"Threatened him? Where? When? Now that really is ridiculous."

"I'm sure it is. But think back. Did you say anything to him at that protest meeting that could have been, I don't know, misinterpreted by somebody who was there, maybe reported inaccurately."

"Just what I told you, about whether he was going to bring in an architect to help him design the mega-monster he was planning to put up next to our house, and that made him turn and walk off to the monster he was still landscaping. Like a wounded child."

"Well that's hardly a threat, for God's sake."

"That was all I said to him that day, I'm certain. Though I did try to make a joke to the group when he walked off that way. I said that young man acted as though I was aiming a gun at his head when I was simply trying to talk sense to him. And then I said I'd choose to shoot his mega-mansion before I'd shoot him, and even if I aimed at that I'd probably miss a target so big. Just a joke."

"You said all that?"

"Well, something like that. I don't remember exactly. And I don't know how many heard. Anyway, nobody seemed to think it was very funny."

"Of course you never know how people are going to take things. And you never know who's in the audience. He may have planted a friend or two in that group to keep an eye out and argue on his side if necessary."

"I don't think so. They all seemed to be on our side. The only friend he had there was his wife, and she didn't say a word."

"Well, her father-in-law thinks those two are having trouble, so I'm surprised she was there."

"Anyway, when we broke up she walked away from the group and just stood there smiling to herself beside her car, at least I think it was her car, smiling I suppose because she thought her husband had put us all in our places at the end with his brilliant farewell speech and his God be with you. I don't think she was smiling at anything I'd said."

"You're probably right about that."

"Well, Christ and the Virgin," Cassie said. "What has happened to free speech in this country if you can't even make a bad joke in public?"

Nick noticed from the start that Detective Masseli's posture was a bit stiffer after he showed up with a young officer in uniform—was it Sergeant Cornfield or Cornfeld?—for his return visit to interview Cassie. With a police buddy there watching the way he conducted himself, he obviously felt less casual than the first time. So why had he brought the Sergeant along anyway? To intimidate Cassie with his look—stocky, less handsome than his superior, but clearly official? Or to be there as a witness to Cassie's presumably shady response to his questions? Whatever the reason, Nick could see that Cassie was already not quite herself, sitting there on the couch with her back rigid and her chin held just a touch higher than usual, no sign of fear but hardly at ease and clearly annoyed. The Sergeant had at least withdrawn to the dining room table and was sitting there with his eyes diverted, as though a bit embarrassed about the way things were going. Detective Masseli, notepad on his thigh, pencil flickering, was gazing steadily at Cassie from the easy chair opposite her. He stopped the pencil suddenly and held it still, tip raised and pointing upward, as if it were a miniature riding crop.

"So your position is that saying you might point a gun at Timothy Parker's head and shoot him was a joke."

"I didn't say I might shoot him," Cassie said. "I just said he acted as though I had a gun pointed at his head. I just didn't like his attitude, so what's all this fuss about nothing?"

"Why would he act the way he acted, I mean turn his back on you and go off in a hurry, unless he considered you some kind of threat?"

"I don't know. You'll have to ask him. Anyway, I don't think he even heard me say anything about a gun. He was already walking away at that point."

"But somebody else heard you. And she, I mean they, heard you say besides this pointing a gun business that you wanted to shoot his house first and then him."

"That's nonsense," Cassie said. "All I said was I'd choose to shoot his house before I'd shoot him, and I wasn't sure I could even hit the house. Huge and awful though it is."

"The point is, dear lady, you said you'd shoot his house before you'd shoot him, which isn't any kind of joke. Especially now that he's disappeared with no trace. At least no trace yet."

"This is ridiculous," Nick said. "Are you trying to suggest that Cassie threatened to shoot Tim Parker's house and then threatened to shoot him and that is why he disappeared?"

"It may be ridiculous to you, but it isn't to us, not when there may be a homicide involved. The point is, we have witnesses that have testified that Mrs. M here was obsessed with Mr. Timothy Parker's house on Independence Road, spoke about it at public meetings, confronted him about it on several occasions, culminating in her threat to shoot it, which she has admitted. So, my friend, you'd better just relax and stay out of this."

"How do you expect him to stay out of it when you say something as, well, as stupid as shooting a house may be homicide?" Cassie said. "Even if the house deserves it, I might add. Honestly, you're wasting your time investigating me."

"I will ignore your insult to me because you're a foreigner and may not always understand the meaning of what I say or the meaning of the language you use, but you'd just better sit up and pay better attention. You may think this business is ridiculous and you may call me stupid, but you're in deep—whatever word you prefer. And it isn't your threat against the house but your threat against Mr. Timothy Parker that has got you there."

"Well that's it," Nick said. "My wife says no more unless there's a lawyer present."

"Just don't you get on your high horse," Detective Masseli said, standing. "You're not a lawyer, you don't know the law here, so you'd just better keep out of this. The only person who has the right to decide when to speak here is Mrs. M herself. And I strongly advise her to tell us anything more she may know before we get involved with lawyers."

"I can't believe it," Cassie said. "It's just like television."

"Television?" Detective Masseli said. "You'd better believe it's not like television."

Cassie lowered her voice to a deep masculine. "You'd better not lawyer up, Mrs. M. Just tell us the truth, the whole truth so help you God, if you want our help. Otherwise, as a former alien, it's likely to be Guantanamo for you."

Detective Masseli sighed. "All right. This has gone far enough. I'm out of here. For the moment. But since our investigation is just beginning, I advise you, Mrs. C, to stay at home and not go traveling anywhere. You can treat this as a big joke at this point in time, but we're not through yet with you and the other witnesses in this case. Not by a long shot."

"Don't worry, Mr. Masseli. I'm not going anywhere. I'm staying right here as long as I can to try to protect my home against natural and human encroachment. If that's the right word."

Detective Masseli moved toward the door. "Did you hear that, Sergeant Cornfeld? Tuck it away. Natural and human encroachment. I suppose we belong to the humans she has in mind. Talk about an attitude regarding law and order in the Township of Princeton."

CHAPTER *Five*

The "unofficial" meeting with once-rowdy and subversive classmate Ron Davis had been more than friendly enough despite the time that had gone by since Nick ran into him at the Dillon Gym pool, the Ronald Whitcomb Davis, Esq. on his office door clearly belonged to a different persona: the lawyer who'd graduated high enough at Columbia Law School to serve a stint in Washington at the Justice Department, then come home to private practice in Lawrenceville. Before they'd gotten down to business that late afternoon, Ron had spent a bit of time reminiscing about the old Liberal Union, now defunct, that the two of them had helped to create during their senior year at Princeton when both of the student political organizations supporting Democrats and Republicans seemed too pallid in their opposition to the Vietnam War. Ron thought it might now be time to revive their undergraduate passion against what was going on in Washington by creating an Old Guard Liberal Union to challenge Bush's wars and Supreme Court appointments, among other sins, but both of them had decided that the name of the proposed club was an oxymoron, and the chance of getting enough so-called liberal people of their generation willing to help fill a lecture hall regularly as a form of late middle-age protest, or whatever you might call it, was really hoping for too much. "I suppose these days it has to be each man and woman behind their own personal barricade," he'd ended up saying. "Which brings me to the issue at hand."

From Ron's point of view, the issue at hand had seemed relatively simple: at this moment in the case, from a legal perspective, there was no strong argument for getting a lawyer officially involved on Cassie's behalf because there was really nothing for a lawyer to work with, no arrest, no court order, nothing but an apparent suspicion by a detective and a suggestion that there might be something more serious down the road as his investigation proceeded. If that were somehow to lead to an indictment after a grand jury examined the evidence before it, then things would be serious indeed—but the only apparent evidence at the moment was testimony presumed to come from the wife of the missing person regarding an overheard threat against that person, and this, in Ron's mind, didn't give the Township justice system sufficient grounds for action against Cassie, including restricting her travel. On the other hand, he felt it made sense for Cassie not to stir things up while an investigation was in progress, in fact to cooperate as much as her conscience allowed, including staying close to home until there was some resolution.

Ron seemed to think that a resolution was likely soon, at least regarding the presumed threat by Cassie and any follow-up concerning her, because it was his guess that the heir to this Solar Estates business would prove to be alive and prospering in another mega-market somewhere. In the end, he'd said, "These people are fruitful and multiply, God bless them, but instead of replenishing the earth, they look first to replenish their pockets, so you and Cassie had better get used to the idea that if Solar Estates doesn't get hold of your teardown, somebody else will in the long run—but that's another issue." The problem at hand? His final advice was that Nick do what he could to track down the Solar Estates heir. That would be one road to a quick resolution, even if it meant talking to Randy Parker about any clue he might have as to why and where his prodigal son may have gone into hiding. "Painful for you surely, old boy, but I'm afraid there is no escaping some pain these days with the mix of dogs at our heels, including a few we elected, right? In any case, I'm here to help if they get too close."

Nick had decided to sacrifice his preference for Lahiere's and offer what used to be called Goodtime Charlie's in Kingston for the midweek lunch he'd arranged with Randy Parker after some soul searching. The restaurant may have changed its name, Charlie Something-else now, and become part of a statewide chain like other local family enterprises, but as far as Nick could remember from his last visit several years ago, the décor and the menu were much the same, as likely as any place in the area to meet Randy's taste. He found more Americana on the walls now—early movie posters, ads for beer long vanished, this and that portrait of bygone Hollywood heroes and heroines, some ripe for nostalgia—yet the aura was still that of a broad-based restaurant that served lonely sports fans watching TV and a few off-hour lingerers in its bar, and beyond that, couples of all ages and whole families in its cluster of booth-lined rooms. And the menu would surely appeal to Randy: rich in steaks, three cuts of prime rib, seven kinds of hamburger, six chicken dishes, a short fish list including Southwest Style Crab Cakes, only Vegetable Ravioli and Chicken Parmigiana touching on the non-American, and a salad bar for free choice—nothing there that might rouse Randy's irony about too much foreign intrusion, though the former name of the place roused his.

Maybe at that point there was little space left for irony anywhere. It hadn't actually surprised him that Randy had agreed so easily to meet for lunch—what did he have to lose, especially when the invitation, offered as coolly as Nick could manage, was to discuss business of concern to both of them? However he interpreted "business," the invitation would surely have struck Randy as some kind of concession, something that put him one step ahead in dealing with this uppity gentleman who'd disdained talking business when they'd last met in Lahiere's. Well, the circumstances were different for both of them now, and Nick had sensed from Randy's tone that he was in an unfamiliar mood: nothing upbeat in it, no excessive reaching out, in fact, no reaching out at all, just a dull, low-key response that seemed to emerge from barely controlled depression.

Of course he had reason to be depressed, both of them did, Tim evidently still missing and Cassie still apparently under suspicion, even if there hadn't yet been any direct follow-up to Detective Marselli's second visit. And the meeting with Ron Davis, ending with a certain optimism about the final outcome, hadn't been exactly reassuring the more he thought about it. What if Tim didn't turn up for a month, two months—or didn't turn up at all? How do you resolve a case involving a missing person when that person simply remains missing? Anyway, at that point, Ron's recommendation that he turn to Randy for whatever he might learn from that source seemed at least plausible now that there wasn't anything else to go on, uncomfortable as the idea appeared at first, and of course resisted by Cassie. How had she put it? What was the point in entering the enemy's tent when there was nothing to negotiate? As far as she was concerned, the only thing they had to offer the man was the unproven fact of her innocence, and since that was an offer of no use to Randy Parker, it would probably just lead to further humiliation.

Exactly what might be of use to Randy Parker, Cassie couldn't say, since she was clearly in no mood to try and analyze any subtleties in his position or trust anything he might offer. You couldn't blame her. From her point of view, no doubt reasonable, he or somebody in his family was obviously responsible for promoting the suspicion that hung over her, and that put him even more squarely in the enemy's camp than he'd already proven himself to be by his hungry eye on their home. When Nick reminded her, only half seriously, that she'd been the one to say know thine enemy, she'd looked up at him from the living room couch in a way that made him turn and go back to his study to gaze out at the spread of leaves now thoroughly covering the backyard lawn with their mix of autumn colors, while barred clouds—how did the poem put it?—bloomed the soft-dying day. He'd looked for the imagined outlines of the garden Cassie said she was planning back there. Now that he thought about it, under this spread of Americana in the former Goodtime Charlie's, maybe the idea of a garden was her quiet way of planting her fiercer sentiments about home into tangible earth, challenging the tiny stretch of no-man's land along the fence next door and highlighting the border of the patch of woods on the other side, while closer to the house—

He felt a touch on the back of his shoulder and turned.

"Let's go for a booth if that's all right by you," Randy said.

"Hi. Sure. The truth is, I'm not very comfortable talking with the bartender patrolling in front of us."

Randy shrugged. "Doesn't bother me. Just more comfortable in a booth. I don't have anything to hide from a bartender or anybody else."

"I don't either. I just don't go for talking sideways. Facing is better."

"Fine by me." Randy said. "Let's talk facing. Though I don't really know what there is to say."

"Well, I have something to say as soon as they get us seated. Anyway, I hope this place is more to your taste than the last place we met, though it isn't quite as simple as it used to be when it was a family business."

"Right. That's the good thing about a family business. Keeping things simple. The problem is keeping a family business together when others are trying to split up the family for their own purposes."

"You think somebody's trying to split up your family? Me and my wife for example?"

"Did I say you were?" Randy said. "I didn't hear myself say that. Of course, others may think that's what's behind this."

"Like who?"

"Like my daughter-in-law, Sheila, for example."

"Your daughter-in-law. All I can say about that—"

The waitress suddenly handed Nick a menu, then Randy, then led them to a booth. She asked about drinks. Randy ordered a double scotch, light on the rocks. Nick said he'd have another glass of chardonnay. He looked at his menu, closed it, then set it down. Randy was studying his with profound interest.

"So what's this about your daughter-in-law?" Nick said.

"Nothing about you personally," Randy said. "Just that she was one of those who heard your wife say she was going to shoot my son's house and then shoot my son."

"That's bullshit. My wife never said that. What she actually said was she'd shoot his house before she'd—never mind."

"Well, I wasn't there. And I'm told you weren't either. But Sheila was. Right there, near enough to hear clearly."

"What was Sheila doing there if I may ask? Just waiting to cause trouble?"

"No. Waiting to drive back home with Tim when his business was done. They work together a lot. Really close. Most of the time. Always on the cell phone to each other. So you can understand why she might take exception to a remark like that and why she's shaken up by what's happened. Not to mention how shaken up I am, my friend."

"Well that goes for me too, my friend. How do you think I feel having my wife accused of homicide when she can't bring herself to swat a fly?"

"Is that so? Well, how do you think I feel when the son I'm working my ass off to get established suddenly disappears? That doesn't much help keeping a simple family business together, does it? My son is my life."

The waitress arrived with the scotch and chardonnay, smiled, set the glasses down, backed off.

"Look," Nick said. "You know as well as I do that my wife's innocent in this business, otherwise you wouldn't have agreed to meet me here. So let's just take that off the table. What I want to suggest is that we work together to find your son. That way both of us can go back to keeping our families, well, let's say intact."

"And just how do you suggest we work together?"

"Let's begin by your telling me your thoughts about what may have made Tim go off suddenly and where he may have gone. Assuming for the moment that it was entirely his decision."

Randy put his glass down. "I have no idea. For a start, I can't assume what you want me to assume. Why would he go off when we'd just about finished one project and were getting ready to start another?"

"That's the question. Maybe something turned him off."

Randy twisted his glass. "The only thing that turned him off was those women coming after him. And my trying to do business with you."

"What business was that?"

"Offering you another chance to review the plans for the house that'll go up next door to yours. And upping the option ante. He didn't like that one bit."

"Is that right? And you don't think that—what shall I call it?— that disagreement may have had something to do with his decision to take off?"

Randy stared at his glass, then took a long swallow. "Tim? Take off for that reason? Not on your life. Take off where?"

"Well that's the basic question," Nick said. "Think about it."

"I'm thinking," Randy said. "I've been thinking. What do you think I've been doing?"

As usual, when there was a need to face decisions calmly, soberly, Cassie tried to invoke whatever of her father's simple faith and insight might bring her peace of mind and help her see things clearly. Now, finally, she remembered him saying to her mother once upon a time, with a wave of his arm: "A garden? Of course we need a garden. Just look outside. Look at the great garden the Holy Virgin has given us whatever the season. A small piece of that will help this girl understand what is honestly beautiful and important." So be it, except that her small piece of the great garden wasn't exactly beautiful these days, many tall trees standing up healthy out front but out back some were crippled and leaning toward the ground or already there, a few bridging the brook where it curved sharply, fallen branches thick where the leaf-covered lawn gave way to the wild acre of unattended land on one side of the lot, the lower portion of it almost a swamp, and this was not the season for the daffodils and snowdrops that the previous owners had planted along the margins.

Still, she was very fond of that wild piece of land that served the open space beyond for its gathering of does and fawns and the occasional buck on his way elsewhere, sometimes a quick fox suddenly angling across the lawn and slithering out of sight in the underbrush by the brook, and the hopping black squirrels everywhere that people said were native to Princeton only, even huge wild turkeys strutting across territory they clearly took to be theirs as long as they chose, and the owls, the silent owls, always two of them sitting side by side on the rotting trunk of an uprooted tree to gaze out tirelessly at the shaded plot in front of them. How much longer would these travelers pass through once a huge mansion rose up next door, no doubt with a fence to protect its back lawn on ground raised with fill to keep it above the stretch of wet plain the two lots now shared. What would happen then on the wet plain that remained when hurricane flooding from the brook came their way? At least she could try to make the narrow passage still tempting enough for a while by planting some new bulbs near the pachysandra, where the lawn drained easily—tulips, crocuses, jonquils, maybe hyacinths, certainly hyacinths, whatever else the book Nick had brought home to help her decide what planting was best in New Jersey at what season, just as soon as she could sit down and focus on her plans for a serious garden.

She'd had the idea before, but it was Nick who pushed for it once she brought it out into the open again, and that had made her take notice, not so much because she suspected he might think it would settle her down and keep her occupied now that she was supposed to stay near home but because it seemed to mean that he'd given up on the idea of retiring early so they could travel without a clear idea of what they would still call home. He hadn't said so, but it didn't make sense for him to suggest that she start a garden in the fall if she would have to abandon it in the spring or even in the summer, not if he was in his right mind, which he surely was even if he seemed to be increasingly angry about the way things were happening in the world outside his study. And now his sudden decision to take a trip to Washington, DC did make her wonder if this Solar Estates business wasn't getting inside him as it had with her.

At first he'd called it just a hunch, then said it was actually more than a hunch—how had he put it?—some combination of hope and

possibility. Whatever you might call it, he'd said finally, he now had reason to think that a trip to Washington might turn things up that could
help him track down Tim Parker and solve the question of his disappearance in a way that would liberate all of them. It was something this
Randy Parker had told him over lunch. The boy was apparently angry
with his father for having promised more than he should have when he
last met with Nick, what his son seemed to think was a kind of bribe,
and the boy had gone off mad. Nick had said that the father couldn't
be sure that was why he'd disappeared or where he'd disappeared to. He
thought it could also be problems the boy was having with his wife, but
he considered his son an idealist, and the last time he'd been on his own
it was to work for the benefit of others by way of a government agency
in the nation's capital, this after going to school at one of the universi-
ties down there and becoming a Christian. That boy a Christian? Pro-
tector of the Virgin's great garden? Not the kind of Christian the world
needed these days as far as she was concerned. Anyway.

Nick had clearly been excited by his new—should she call it his
new mission or his new adventure?—in any case his chance, as he put
it, to act rather than sit around waiting for things he couldn't control
to happen to the two of them. And she was grateful for that. But she
felt there must have been a bit of liberation for him in taking a train
out of town to the place he'd grown up. May the gods go with him
and may they bring him safely home. For her part, her bit of liberation
had begun as soon as she'd dropped Nick off at the Princeton Junction
station on the southbound side. Straight back to Amy's, and the two
of them off for lunch at the Ferry House. If that was a violation of the
detective's "suggestion" that she stay close to home, she didn't give a
damn. She was going to go wherever she wanted to in her hometown,
which is the way she chose to interpret his warning, if that was the right
word. Anyway, what could that poor detective do to her? Handcuff her

to the carport column? Just let him try.

And out again tonight, up to Palmer Square to join the protest against Bush's war, if that really turned out to amount to anything, and after that, wherever Amy decided it would be fun to have a drink or two with the organizers, including a few of the younger generation working hard to enlist undergraduates. Palmer Square did have its amusing side in a way. She remembered that one of the local writers had written that at this season, with the days short and the nights long, Palmer Square and the ivy-covered University buildings across the street had become a kind of lit-up theme park. True enough, charming in its way, but not the whole story. Another thing she remembered was her young cousin's visit from Athens, taking him to what was then a Greek restaurant on Witherspoon Street, and the cousin asking, when the place emptied at 9:30 like most other restaurants in town, whether it wasn't time to head for the town square to catch a bit of the local action, and she, desperately trying to keep a straight face, driving him around a totally vacant Palmer Square, then the quiet West End, then slowly back home. The next day her cousin had asked permission to head for New York City. Of course. He was so young. How could she refuse?

Anyway, the quiet, the slow pace of the town, those were things she'd liked about it from the beginning. People living there left you alone, they didn't crowd you, and there was always something to do if you had the heart for it—music, theatre, lectures, even if she usually hated lectures. And time to read if you planned your life right. Most of all, time to sit down and eat with friends, whether out on the town or at home, your choice. So why was she beginning to feel hemmed in again?

It wasn't only this business with the detective. She could probably go on moving around town as desired. It was her feeling that she no longer had full control of where her life was headed—where their life was headed. And it wasn't pressure from Nick. He seemed to have no more control over what might lie ahead for them than she did. Somehow things were being decided for both of them, decided from the outside. And it wasn't what her mother would have called Fate or the Will of God or some other hidden force. Her father would have been closer to the truth: whatever the ancients may have thought, it isn't the gods, it's men who create the big problems, bad government, bad investment, poverty, wars, sometimes simply human beings who thought they were gods. And here, in this small corner of the world, she knew the hemming in was mostly human, others deciding how you should live, the developers, some members of the local government, of course a share of the elected politicians, all those ambitious operators and even well-meaning climbers of one kind or another, and those whose threatening passions stifled your own. But if she tried to get out of that circle, get free, where could she go?

Nick could no longer rouse much nostalgia as he headed for the place he'd once considered his hometown during his father's brief tour in Washington at the Treasury Department in the early Sixties and his three years at Wilson High. In his younger days he'd found excuses to go back there fairly regularly, before he went abroad, before Cassie and their Grand Tour, but he realized the last time he'd been in Washington was at his fortieth high school reunion, an event that had bored Cassie speechless and had made him feel his age with a certain lingering melancholy. The old buddies from his locker room and back booth days were mostly gray haired and potbellied, some still obsessed with the Redskins, others with local problems, few with national politics, and the girls—oh those gorgeous, unapproachable, bobby-socked teasers, and the others with a soft heart under rigid nipples who'd emerge with swollen lips from half a night of necking but more or less secure below the waist—so tempting, so delicious back then but now with much of the sweetness gone from the eyes, the voices almost sexless, the conversations protected, close to formal.

And the one girl, the one woman, who ended up breaking his heart back then but who might have brought substance to his nostalgia wasn't planning to come to this reunion or any other for reasons unexplained to the planners, Vicky of reading Dickens together and visiting what culture the city had to offer, Vicky of the long nights and sober talks and love that managed to survive on petting and promises unrealized in the end, Vicky who was wise beyond her years and gentle in finding a way to give him back his frat pin because, she said, she didn't want to violate the trust between them as she was afraid she would, Vicky at least partially in love with somebody else, somebody older, too proud to carry along another younger suitor simply because he was good to her, worshiped her, was ready to learn more from her than anybody else in those days about what was honorable and what wasn't, what excitement there was in seeing things and knowing things from reading and viewing that he couldn't have discovered on his own.

His disappointment in not finding Vicky at that reunion surely influenced his posture with her sorority sisters who'd shown up. He must have seemed to them as they to him: a dull ghost of what he once was suddenly passing through town only to vanish again into oblivion the next day. Still, that visit had served to revive images of what had seemed to matter greatly once upon a time, young images of longing and loss that he'd then taken back north with him to put away in the mind's back drawer along with other faded remnants of feeling.

Yet if nostalgia was at best a flitting part of it, the trip to Washington had ended up the best prospect for making a move when his choices had become so limited that any reasonable excuse—what he'd done his

best to explain to Cassie as a strong hunch about where Tim Parker may
have headed—seemed preferable to squatting on his haunches, waiting
for the unidentified moment to do something, finally letting others have
their way with his life. And now that the train had eased out of Balti-
more and was barreling south, he'd actually begun to feel some excitement creeping in to counter the somber mood of recent days. One thing
no longer bothered him: whether or not he should have tried to follow
his first impulse and work somehow through the local democratic process in Princeton to demonstrate how vulnerable, how undemocratic,
Cassie's situation now appeared to be, how much it apparently had to do
with her effort to challenge those who wanted to impose their sense of
progress on her well-established contentment, along with her legitimate
activity as a citizen concerned about the environment, even if admittedly
with a personal issue at its heart.

Thinking about that democratic process had finally defeated him
after he'd done some research and had learned that the various first-level
boards and committees and commission he might scout for help with
an appeal against the authorities were all appointed by the Township,
ultimately with the approval of the Mayor. Some were considered to
be hard-working, some not, but each was only accountable first of all
to itself and then to the Township Committee. The best account of the
process came from the one board chairman he'd managed to track down
by phone. "You've got the whole thing wrong," the guy said. "We don't
represent you or anybody else. We don't take up personal cases. And
we don't legislate. We take up issues, of course, but we simply advise
the Township Committee as requested. It's the Committee that acts. If
you want change, if you want to appeal something legislated, if you
want ordinances reviewed and maybe revised, get yourself elected to the
Committee."

Right, so along with four others, he could choose the Mayor, the ultimate leader, under some divine grant of choice. What would you call that kind of top-down governance if you weren't living where your money in all shapes tells you In God We Trust? Anyway, there was clearly no possibility of getting anywhere through that mostly self-accountable bureaucracy to the grand level of the Township Committee to make his case for an ordinary citizen who'd been maligned by a false witness, this presumably at the next Committee meeting under "Comments from the Audience" late in the agenda when he could stand up to confront a wall of silent, no doubt ambivalent, faces in order to plead his wife's innocence.

And what would he say? That his wife was under suspicion because of an accusation apparently spread by commercial parties out to promote their project of re-developing the long-settled and sylvan Queenston Park with giant mansions often made of prefabricated modules covered by a veneer of brown-stained shingles and thin dark stones on high mounded ground entered by broad asphalt driveways with ample plaza space for guest parking, the uprooted lot fenced in and prettied up by sod and shrubs and baby pines to distract the eye from the stumps of ancient trees now departed and the mind from the prospect ahead of more flooding and less sunlight for neighbors too close for their comfort, along with the various creatures who used to hunt for food or simply take their pleasure in passing safely under an open patch of sky to an increasingly swampy stretch of shaded land? Christ. What would be the point of that kind of rhetoric, even if there was truth in it? The silent faces would have heard the best part of it already, several times over, and they knew perfectly well who profited most from this progress in town planning and who least. Besides, a personal complaint expressed in such an unofficial way against parties presumably doing their business with a proper permit? Excuse me, not this Committee's territory.

The more he'd thought about it, what Randy Parker had finally come up with at their lunch opened an increasingly plausible possibility about where that irate son of his might be hiding out. The first clue Randy had given him, which he reported to Cassie, was based on an image of the boy going off to brood in his pup tent somewhere near his DC college because he was full of wrath at the old man for what he took to be an attempt to earn the Mandevilles' favor by bribing them. But the second clue was subtler and didn't surface at first: Randy's comment that the boy was apparently fed up with working in what he considered to be a hostile community led by a group of loud-mouthed men and women of leisure, old-guard types in his book, who were against any kind of advancement, financial or comfort-wise, even if it was clearly to the personal benefit of most of them in the long run, anyway those who *had* a long run. What Tim wanted to know, according to Randy, was why didn't these aging protesters focus on supporting housing for seniors in condominium-style developments and leave the younger generation to move ahead with the promotion of superior family-friendly living in single homes, the larger the families, the larger the homes. The whole thing was finally a matter of principle, Randy had said, a matter of your basic philosophy. How had he put it? "That boy's the thinker in the family. Always was in a way. The greatest good for the greatest number in a free-wheeling society is his motto. Liberty, equality, and so forth. You know what I'm talking about?"

The man had become all wound up, taken off on the history of his son's transformation from an ordinary adolescent slob to a Christian who believed in service to his fellow man, not in the uptight Catholic way that maybe had started him down that road during his college years at Georgetown, but in the individual way that had emerged from his conversion to a kind of evangelical belief in his own worth and his special relation to God, *you know what I mean?* Right, and his service? Well, for a start, not in the military, thank God, but on the advice of some priest of a teacher, a failed stab at the Foreign Service, which was supposed to be Georgetown's specialty, so who can say why he failed to make it along that route. But all things work for those who know how to play the odds, right? Tim then looked into several of the government agencies that were recruiting new blood after eight years of the giveaway Clinton administration and the promising arrival of George W., and taking a cue from the old man—Randy's first smile of the hour—he'd interviewed at HUD where Randy had what you might call a connection or two. And that's where the boy had ended up for a spell after his graduation, this program and that—who can remember such details?—eventually specializing in what became something called the Hope VI program for replacing obsolete public housing with updated private dwellings. Not bad training in a way, Randy had to admit, but hardly competition for the partnership in Solar Estates he was able to offer the boy after he'd married Sheila in DC and shown his parents that he'd really settled down. But what was all that worth now? Randy had lowered his eyes: "I mean, the poor son of a bitch."

Well, maybe yes, and maybe no. As far as Nick was concerned, Gatsby he wasn't, nor likely to become. More an updated Tom Buchanan, nibbling at the edge of a new set of stale ideas. Anyway, Randy had provided what could prove to be the essential clue, even if he'd remained clueless himself. Where was this neo-idealistic boy likely to head if he was not only fed up with his old man and his wheeler-dealer ways but also with what he saw as this community of old farts and their aging women that he was forced to cater to in central New Jersey? Surely some place where he felt more at home, a place of good beginnings where enough people thought the way he did and where he'd made some useful connections himself—not to mention where he had found his God and his wife—a place where he'd learned what his version of free enterprise was all about these days and where there might still be possibilities he'd once passed up. The place seemed fairly obvious. Anyway, whatever thin mist of nostalgia might still be coloring Nick's vision of where he was headed, he decided he was aiming in the right direction, in fact the only reasonable direction for finding a way out for Cassie's sake but also for his own.

When the dining clubs on Prospect Avenue were back in the local news about damage done during a drinking spree, Cassie remembered Nick explaining that Prospect Avenue was what the undergraduates called Prospect Street in his day, or more intimately, just The Street, and it was probably given its official name because at one time, who knows how long ago, it must have offered a prospect of Lake Carnegie and the farmland beyond from the high point of the ridge that ran from the edge of the campus halfway to Kingston. But whatever its early history, the street's famous name struck Cassie as rather out of tune with reality these days, given that, at the University end at least, the street was crowded on both sides by grand mansions of varied style with no view at all up front except the prospect of each other.

During all her years in Princeton, she'd never been inside one of these dining clubs for undergraduates called eating clubs. Nick had belonged to one of them while in college—she couldn't remotely remember which—but had never been back there since they'd settled in the town because he said he'd come to see the clubs of his day as mostly extra-curricular training centers for snobbery, envy, anti-intellectual prejudices, and discrimination of one kind or another, beginning with a selection process called Bicker—apparently brief private interviews of potential new members by a group of old members focusing on the way the candidate looked, talked, and reviewed his social or school background—this carrying over into a classification system of preference that was passed on from one generation to the next. Cassie had been amused. In America? Without a king and his court to establish a model for such inherited nobility and its courtly manners?

Nick had told her that since his day, especially after women were admitted to the University, all but a few of the clubs had gone in for open admission, whatever that meant exactly, but he'd added that along with the clubs that remained selective, there was still enough room to practice exclusivity off The Street in the growing number of what he called undercover fraternities and sororities, about which he and his fellow alumni knew little. She'd seen older generations of members using the club backyards for parking and picnicking at football games, and she assumed some of them gathered at the club bars to revive a certain memory of their youth before heading home. In any case, there had never been that sort of thing in her Princeton life, especially since she had little interest in American football and its various rituals even if Nick—odd, when she thought about it—was still an aficionado of that rather violent sport and sometimes took her along to what he called this or that "important home game." But from another perspective, she was intrigued by Amy's invitation to join her for a drink at one of the clubs while she worked briefly with its president on some kind of environmental petition. Why not? She was still young enough to want to learn something new from the younger generation and their ways, a thing Nick apparently satisfied year in and year out in the classrooms and corridors of his teaching. Anyway, since she was ten years younger than he was, she was not likely to be looked at from the same distance by that generation. The environmental petition wasn't finished yet and therefore not public, but she didn't press Amy to see it in draft. She could wait on that. Just getting out of the house for a bit was appealing, bored as he was waiting at home yet another night for Nick to return.

One problem had been what to wear. Amy had said dress was casual, the occasion strictly informal, just a chance for her to meet whatever club officers were still around as the fall break was about to start. Her friend was among the more conscientious, planning to spend part of the break getting his act together as head of a student environmental committee that was doing what it could to see that environmental issues had priority in the University's proposed expansion. What exactly "casual" meant on The Street, Cassie couldn't imagine. All she'd ever seen of dress for social occasions at the University end of Prospect Avenue was tall and slender girls in tight dark dresses walking sometimes a bit awkwardly in high heels beside even taller dark-suited partners—could they possibly have been wearing tuxedos?—on their way to serious partying somewhere along that street in deep springtime. She didn't want to show Amy her total ignorance by asking questions. And there was the business of trying to be inconspicuous when venturing outside the house.

She'd decided it was time to ignore that business. If she was being watched, which she really doubted, it wasn't close enough to give her any sense of it, so why give it another thought? And she'd settled some time since for simply wearing a scarf around her head and dark glasses when she went out to walk in the neighborhood or head uptown. To-night, since Amy was doing the driving and she in the passenger's seat free to turn her back a bit on the side window, she'd decided to let her hair fall uncovered down to her shoulders. She'd chosen a green blouse unbuttoned low enough to show off her gold chain necklace, a straight black skirt, black suede shoes, the whole meant to make her look both a touch fashionable and a touch informal, if still basically conservative. Amy had shown up wearing a navy blue pin-striped suit, black turtle-neck, and a pearl necklace. She would have looked elegant if she weren't carrying a file folder that hid her purse and gave her something of a professorial aura.

They'd found a parking place almost outside the club, which was one of the largest on the street—"I'd say sort of Colonial red brick mixed with something else, wouldn't you say?" Amy said. Cassie thought it had a quaint name for a building that huge: Cottage Club. Once they were in the foyer, more like a narrow living room that ran the length of the building, the cottage turned out to have a hollow center that consisted of a grand brick patio, crossed on the second floor at the outer end by a balustraded balcony that led from a giant window on one side to a giant window—or was that a door imitating a window?—on the other side. Amy's friend, Dwight came up to greet them in the vestibule and hung their coats over his arm. He seemed younger than Cassie had expected, blond, broad-shouldered, all smiles. He squeezed Amy's free arm—she smiled back rather stiffly—and turned, beaming, to Cassie.

"Welcome to this side of paradise," he said, shaking her hand, then touching her waist, lightly, quickly. "Not that anybody around here really reads that book any more, good as it is, if hardly Fitzgerald's best, even if it made this place famous. Have you read *This Side of Paradise?*"

"Have I read that book?" Cassie said. "No. Should I?"

"Don't bother. Pretty much out of date, really. Some good moments. Anyway, that was another Princeton. I quote from memory: 'They filled the Jewish youth's bed with lemon pie.' That's a direct quote, can you believe it? Great fun, right? People swallowing goldfish and that kind of thing."

"Goldfish? Why goldfish for heaven's sake?" Amy asked.

"Just to show off," Dwight said. "Idiotic. Though not as dangerous as playing Russian roulette. Blinded one undergraduate back then. A lot of students weren't serious in those days."

"And now they are?" Cassie said.

"Some are, some aren't," Dwight said. "Most are. In their way. You really have to be pretty serious, given the competition. Let me hang up the coats and I'll be right back."

Cassie took Amy's arm. They walked to the windows that gave on the patio.

"Handsome boy," Cassie said. "Likes to talk."

"Well, he's a senior," Amy said. "Talk is one thing they really teach them to do in this place. Anyway, he's quick, a bit ambitious, a bit pushy, but otherwise harmless, and I find him quite useful. A hard worker for the right causes."

"Such as?"

"Well, as I said, the environment for a start. Which ties in with our next approach to the Township Committee. I've seen him show up at our local meetings sometimes, I suppose mainly because he's writing a senior thesis on the structure of small-town government in New Jersey. He knows his history. And he's had experience in several protest movements, which is why I'm counting on him to get our petition statement right. And also why I'm thinking of using him in my campaign if I decide to run for the Township Committee. That is, once he graduates."

"You're thinking of running for the Township Committee?"

Amy put two fingers to Cassie's lips. "Shush. Too early to say."

Dwight came up smiling. "Let's go next door, ladies. I've tried to make it comfortable for having a drink before Amy and I get down to work, but there's nobody around to help this close to the break. I've cornered a table in there for those of us over twenty-one who haven't already gone home. That comes down to me and our Treasurer, Terry Hopper. Rooms with me upstairs. We're the ones in charge, so to speak. He'll be down in a minute."

Cassie thought the room next door something close to grotesque: about the size of a normal living room in a mansion, with a fireplace in the center of one long wall, a spread of large windows on the smaller wall facing the street, a huge portrait of a tiger lounging on a sand dune over the fireplace mantel, the remaining space on the sides of the fireplace and the long wall opposite decorated with what struck her as a picture gallery of British recreation, upscale and otherwise: a polo game in progress, *The Finish at Henley*, a rough moment of rugby, a generous taste of cricket, and over the piano in one corner, another tiger, much smaller, looking very tame. Dwight led them to a card table in the center of the room. It was covered by a mildly stained tablecloth, an open bottle of white wine in the middle beside a row of water glasses, a dish of peanuts beside that.

"You'll have to forgive the amenities," Dwight said. "Since Terry and I decided to let the staff go home early, we had to make do as best we could. Wine OK with everybody? Good."

He poured wine into four water glasses a third of the way up. He smiled.

"Somebody in your club loves England," Cassie said. "And no scenes of American football or baseball on the walls?"

"Just tradition," Dwight said. "Somebody donated all that stuff who knows when. Nobody got around to changing it."

"Not even F. Scott Fitzgerald?" Amy said. "Anyway, you should have his picture up there instead of that tiger lounging on a beach."

"I suppose. Anyway, from the club point of view, Fitzgerald was a problem. The word is, he got thrown out of the club sometime after he left Princeton, without graduating by the way, thrown out of his beloved Cottage Club because he came down here with his crazy wife to serve as chaperones and showed up drunk wearing a halo and wings and carrying a lyre. Too much for the puritan crowd of those days. Sad story, really."

"So the club is no longer puritan?" Cassie said. "But it's still selective, right?"

Dwight studied her. "Doesn't mean all that much any more. Just tradition. There are plenty of places on The Street for those who don't want to be selective. Besides, the University is trying to shift over completely to the college system like Yale and Harvard. But don't hold your breath. That was a plan Woodrow Wilson had for Princeton at the beginning of the last century. Seriously."

"But this club still selects some who want to join and rejects others who want to join, isn't that so?" Cassie said. "I don't mean to raise an issue. I just wonder on what basis people are selected."

"Well, it's a bit difficult to explain. Congeniality. Accomplishment. Like friends you went to school with. Maybe friends in power. You know. The usual."

"What about politics?" Amy said.

"Politics? Again, that depends mostly on friends—"

"I don't mean club politics. Party affiliation. Family political background. How people vote."

"How people vote? A lot don't vote. Most people here are too busy for politics these days, sad to say. It isn't like Europe, if that's what you have in mind. Protests and that kind of thing. Unless of course there's a draft."

"A draft?" Cassie said.

"You know, Selective Service. Conscription. Which I personally would strongly oppose. So would most others here. More interested in other kinds of service. A draft would bring out the protesters, no question. Where is Terry? I'll be right back."

Dwight got up, smiled, went out the doorway.

"I didn't mean to be difficult," Cassie said. "At least I didn't ask if money was involved in this selection business. I mean family money."

"I don't think so much in this club," Amy said. "Maybe in one or two of the others. Anyway, Dwight's very middle class. Bright and all that, they all are, but he never speaks of his family. He's what people call very likable, very cool. And he seems to be good at knowing the right people. Which is why he ought to go far if he gets into politics professionally. But he's still so very young. I mean—"

Dwight appeared in the doorway and ushered his friend Terry through ahead of him. Terry was tall—six three, six four—thick dark hair low on his forehead, heavy eyebrows, high cheekbones, dark stubble below. Cassie thought he looked at least four or five years older than Dwight. She also thought he would look diabolic if he didn't have those clear blue eyes that stayed sharply focused on what they were looking at: her face, even after he shook hands and sat down opposite her.

"Ladies, sorry I'm late," he said. "Overslept this morning and had to get myself organized this afternoon."

"Terry tends to sleep a lot," Dwight said. "Says he's making up for time he lost in the Marines. Not to mention after."

"You served in the Marines?" Amy asked.

"Two years. Discharged with a bad kidney just as I was heading out to Iraq. Two years of lost time for myself and my country. And a few following that, to clear my head. Anyhow, plenty of opportunity now for us older folk to catch up on lighter living in beautiful central New Jersey, don't you think? Even in college."

Cassie heard a light southern accent behind the slow quiet mocking tone. He reached for the bottle of wine and filled her water glass beyond the halfway point.

"That's too much for me," Cassie said. "I don't drink without eating. An old Greek habit, I'm afraid."

"You're Greek?" Dwight asked. "I mean originally?"

"Originally and still. In a way," Cassie said.

Terry was gazing at her again. "Let's drink to the Greeks. Some of my best friends are Greeks. Marine Greeks, that is, not fraternity Greeks. And I can tell you I put in some good time in Athens on my European tour. Spent two years just traveling around over there to get myself back into civilization once my kidney problem improved. Loved Paris espe-

cially. Bistro crawling. That kind of thing. Not to mention *les femmes.*
Awesome. So anyhow, let's drink to the Greeks."

He raised his glass. Dwight raised his. Amy turned slightly sideways
and didn't raise hers. Cassie shrugged and raised hers.

"Why not? But that won't get me to drink without eating."

"Have a peanut," Terry said.

He passed the dish. Cassie popped one in her mouth, then pushed
the dish away.

"Terry's a mathematical genius," Dwight said. "I'm not kidding. He's
not our Treasurer for nothing. The guy's got a mind like a calculator."

"Just practice," Terry said. "Most anybody can be a calculator if they
try hard enough."

Cassie found his image confusing: a humble statement delivered
with a dismissive gesture that suggested arrogance. He was looking at
her again.

"Whatever," Dwight said. "Let me ask you guys, would you mind
if Amy and I had ten minutes to go over the wording of a petition she's
working on and one I'm working on, mine having to do with University policy regarding trees and open space. Amy knows more about that
kind of thing than anybody in this town. So we can sit in the kitchen
back there where there's a table and do our bit for humanity. Then
maybe we can like roll out for dinner somewhere."

"It's all right by me," Terry said. "I'm sure Cass and I can entertain
ourselves. Even if she doesn't drink much without serious eating."

"Do you mind?" Amy said to Cassie, picking up her file folder. "I
think these petitions are important. And I promise to be no more than
ten minutes or so."

"Why should I mind?" Cassie said. "Terry here can tell me about the
Greeks he knew in the Marines. Or whatever, as they say these days."

Dwight stood up and waited behind Amy's chair. She got up slowly, glanced at Cassie, tucked the file folder under her arm, glanced at Terry, turned toward the door.

Dwight pushed her chair back in place. "We'll be back before you miss us."

Terry watched him guide Amy out the door. He sat up from his slouch suddenly and leaned forward, his elbows on the table. He seemed on the verge of smiling.

"Well," he said. "Here we are. Mind if I get a little cozier? Easier to talk that way. I'm really very shy. Especially with women older than me. I mean I have a thing about good-looking women your age, whatever it may be exactly."

He got up and moved to Dwight's chair. When he leaned towards her, Cassie eased her chair back. She brought her legs out from under the table and crossed them.

"I suppose I could be flattered by a remark like that," she said. "But I'm not. It makes me uncomfortable."

Terry shook his head. "There's no need to be uncomfortable. I'm just trying to be friendly. Even if I have to admit that I find you, how shall I put it? Mysteriously attractive."

"Look," Cassie said. "Where I come from we sometimes get married young enough for me to be your mother, as the saying goes. Easily. So get serious."

"I'm serious," Terry said. "Really serious. These arguments about age just don't touch me. When I'm attracted, I'm attracted. Can't help it. It's as simple as that."

He reached forward abruptly and put his hand on her knee. When she tried to brush it away, he held tight. The hint of a smile was gone. He removed his hand, then brought it back to ease it under the lip of her dress.

Cassie stood up. She reached down and patted Terry's cheek.

"I should slap your face," she said. "But you're so immature, however old you are, so what's the point."

"You'd better not try," Terry said. "I'd break your arm."

"I bet you would." Cassie said. "You're just stupid enough to do a thing like that. Even if you are a mathematical genius. Which I doubt."

She turned and walked out as casually as she could manage. She decided not to take time to look for Amy in the kitchen. As she headed for the front door coat closet, she saw Terry standing in the doorway of the room they'd been in. She avoided looking at his face. She found her coat and went outside without putting it on. There was a low moon rising, not quite full, blood orange. She put on her coat and headed home down Prospect Avenue. It was turning cold.

CHAPTER *Six*

Nick smiled to himself. Tracking down Jackson Ripaldo to solve the problem of access to the Housing and Urban Development building on 7th Street, SW, had been an inspiration, a friendly gesture by one or the other of the gods who apparently still winged across the nation's capital and its Hellenic-style monuments even on a chilly November morning. It was most likely Dionysus in view of the weakness for resinated wine that he and Jackson shared, or maybe some other more local deity responsible for Jackson's gift of fertility, another son fairly recently with his second wife, Lotte, later in the couple's middle-aged romance than anybody would have thought possible. Strictly a sober family man these days, he'd told Nick when he finally got him on the phone, Jackson's tone of voice still carrying enough remnant irony to make the sobriety claim suspicious. But the trace of irony was gone when he added that his return to full family life was easy when it was handled by a lady as skillful and lovely as the one he'd brought back with him from Austria, the grand reward that made up for his failed campaign to out the Big W, as he called the former Austrian President and UN Secretary, or more elaborately, the recently deceased master hypocrite and cunning amnesiac of the vanished Wehrmacht.

From the one evening he'd spent with the Ripaldo couple, Nick had to agree that the lady was a tenacious beauty: white-haired, face sculpted gracefully if showing the lines of a certain age, but the body twenty years younger. And that voice—close enough to Dietrich's to rouse the ghostly sound of Hollywood's onetime favorite German playgirl. Jackson, muckraking swinger of the days they'd traveled together during one or another European summer before he met Cassie, had lucked out in the end, and who would say he hadn't earned some peace of mind after years of walking along the edge of this or that risky conflict in the name of justice, sober or not.

Fortunately the old boy hadn't lost his talent for imposture in pursuing a necessary story or an unnecessary pleasure, which he claimed had got him through a number of roadblocks as a cub reporter pretending to be an official member of one or another American mission operating abroad, and later, into some kind of serious trouble during his failed effort to challenge Waldheim's rise from atrocity planner to head of the Austrian state. Jackson hadn't hesitated more than a minute when Nick finally got into the details of what had brought him unannounced to Washington. They were sitting on the terrace of his friend's renovated house in Georgetown, with just enough distant view of the Potomac to make it seem the right place for an urban sailor still living off the memory of grander waters.

"So let me get this straight," Jackson had said. "There's a family of megabuilders in Princeton trying to ease you out of your home first by trying to buy you out and then by intimidating you with the false accusation that your wife is responsible by way of certain threatening language for the withdrawal from the business and disappearance of the family's son and heir. Only you think he hasn't disappeared at all but is alive and well and hiding out in Washington as we speak, probably working for HUD, where he once worked as a neo-conservative youth trying to convert public housing into private housing in a faithful neo-conservative way, right?"

"Well, summarizing the thing like that, you make it sound a bit less complicated and more unreal than it actually is, though I admit it's seemed unreal enough at times. Especially when a detective arrives at your house and tells your wife that she would do well to stay close to home until they've thoroughly investigated an accusation by the wife of the man who disappeared that my wife had threatened to kill him."

"Yea, I can see how that would be cause for serious discomfort. Did the detective claim to have any evidence beside this woman's testimony?"

"No. He wasn't talking. It came down to what Cassie was reported to have said in public at some point during a confrontation with the son and heir, as you call him, who apparently became miffed when Cassie suggested he bring in an architect to help him before he created another wounded monster."

"Wounded?"

"Well, maybe that's my addition. A huge McMansion that looks as though it has a broken hunk of arm sticking out of it. I won't elaborate. And when this hotshot son took off in a huff, she said something out loud about his acting as if she had a gun pointing at his head when in fact she would shoot the man's creation before she'd shoot the man himself, though she doubted she could hit the mansion from where she was standing despite how large and awful it was."

"Huh?"

"A joke. Maybe a bad joke, but it so happens the son and heir's wife heard it, and maybe some others, who knows how it was reported, and anyway the guy disappeared right after this public confrontation. And since the detective apparently didn't have much else to work with, he focused on this presumed threat that Cassie made in front of a group of her fellow protesters."

"Aha," Jackson said. "Protesters. There's a clue. Very dangerous word while we have a war on. Whatever war we've gotten ourselves into. Middle East, Far East, Beltway political, the visible and invisible war on terror, the various battles between competing heavenly hosts of various religions. Cassie should be more careful. Whether it's Big Brother or maybe even Big Sister in power down here, you're being watched. Bad jokes will not be tolerated. Good jokes will be tolerated even less. Remember, old boy, you—"

"OK. OK. The point is, those people not having any real evidence is what worries me."

"What people?"

"Some of the people running my beautiful hometown. Unless I'm just being paranoid after what we've had to deal with recently, it probably means there are people up there searching for ways to keep Cassie and her friends from interfering with local progress."

"Progress? Another dangerous word. What progress?"

"Commercial progress, expanded construction possibilities, real estate development, providing opportunity for changing the town into a serious megalopolis. But if we find this Tim Parker, maybe we can at least free ourselves of phony accusations and barricade ourselves in our own modest home to better fight off the giant invaders."

"Well, that makes perfect sense. I guess. Anyway, I'm here to help you, old buddy. Still ready to take on whatever rough beast comes slouching in to destroy our sense of the good life, yours and mine in particular. So let's work out a plan. To begin with, you're sure this guy is working for HUD? I'd say it isn't all that easy to get back to an old job in the government once you're out, but what do I know?"

"The point is, it's our best starting point. His father said the boy worked hard to make contacts when he was in that job, and he's bound to have friends in the government there and beyond as a young neo-conservative warrior returned to the battle."

The plan Jackson came up with had sounded simple enough: he would pretend to be writing up the HUD program called Hope VI for the local Georgetown paper he contributed to every now and then, and once he had an interview set up at the HUD building on 7th Street, it would be a piece of cake. They'd send a secretary down to escort him past the guard and up to an office or conference room or wherever, and if he couldn't get to the list of those working in the building from the secretary—hardly plausible that he wouldn't, even if he did say so himself—he'd con the information out of the guy he was interviewing. After all, Jackson said, despite the metal detector and the escort business, HUD wasn't a secret agency except maybe occasionally when it had some kind of hidden agenda. One way or another, he'd find out if this Timothy Parker was on the payroll, and once he had that news, he'd make the interview perfunctory so Nick wouldn't have to cool his butt too long downstairs walking the entrance hallway.

So why was it taking him this long? Jackson had been his usual audacious self on their way into the building, stroking the guard on duty with a full and learned review of the Redskins' recent games while he waited for the escort lady to arrive, and when she turned out to be a reasonably handsome fifty plus, the old charmer put his arm around her waist to guide her ahead of him into the elevator a good long unnecessary slice of time before the elevator door actually opened. If Jackson was his old self, they should be working together by now, political pals, co-conspirators, who knew what sudden convenient engagement.

One thing that hadn't been discussed was exactly what they were to do if Tim Parker turned out to be there in the building and took umbrage at being hunted down. In the old days, the ripe and limber scuba days that had served their rebellious self-confidence as bachelors, they could have handled him and any healthy young HUD operators he might choose to drag along simply by the right kind of threatening gestures, but nowadays? He'd suggested that if the guy was found, they might try to move ahead by maybe taking Tim out for a drink and a more or less civilized conversation about the need for him to call off his conniving wife and any other intruding friends of his up in Princeton. Ripaldo had thought that over for a minute, made a face, said nothing. Anyway, given what Tim Parker had shown himself to be in public, just where was that kind of diplomacy likely to lead? And given Ripaldo's silent response, how could you know just how far he'd moved beyond the civil and not-so-civil disobedience days that had brought them together? Still, if he actually found the boy working upstairs, well, that would solve the first and most important problem. Beyond that—

"You gonna wear out your shoes if you keep pacing that way," the guard said from his desk seat. "Why don't you get yourself a coffee or a beer around the corner? I'll send your friend after you if he shows up while you're gone."

"Thanks. I expect he'll be down in a minute. And I need the exercise."

"Well, we all need exercise, that's right. But you wearing a frown gonna give you a bad head before long. I'd say it might do yourself some good to have a drink. Not meaning to intrude."

Nick smiled. "You've got a point. Where can I get a drink close by?"

"That depends on what you're looking for, I mean where and what and what for. The boys here generally go over to the Foggy Bottom Brew Pub at the L'Enfant Plaza Hotel around the back here across the way. But I never been there myself. Too high class for me, if you know what I mean. Pricewise."

"Maybe I'll just try singing to myself as I walk. Cure the frown that way. Only I can't find much to sing about these days."

"None of us can, my friend. And I don't have to tell you why, I'm sure."

"That you don't," Nick said. "Anyway, thanks for the advice, and here's my friend. So I guess I'll go for a drink after all."

Jackson was still escorted, this time by a white-haired lady clearly of an advanced age in his book, and he didn't look happy, though he saluted the guard casually in passing, then turned and shook the lady's hand. Coming out of the entrance hall into the dusk, he didn't say a word until well outside.

"The guy you're looking for doesn't work in there," he said, taking Nick's arm. "At least they claim they have no record of his working there. Which of course may not be the same thing."

"Meaning what?" Nick said.

"Meaning they're not about to tell me one way or another. The receptionist didn't have his name on her list or couldn't find it after looking for it a bit too casually. And when they finally let me in to talk to the cone-head who was presumably in charge up there, he said he'd never heard of the man. Only he said it as though he was lying through his teeth."

"Why would he do that?"

"Maybe because he'd been told to do that. Maybe by this Timothy Parker. Maybe by somebody else higher up."

"Well HUD isn't exactly the CIA. I mean, as you said, it isn't a secret agency. Unless you know more than you're telling me."

"It isn't the CIA but it's still a Washington operation. These days you aren't anybody in this town if you haven't got some secrets or if you aren't in a position to cover for somebody. And lying? Especially when the press is coming through the door? I mean you—"

"All right. So what do we do now?" Nick asked.

"Well let's go have a drink and figure it out. On the way there I can fill you in on what the Hope VI program does for the public good these days, such as—let me see what I've scribbled here—such as changing the physical shape of public housing and placing public housing in non-poverty neighborhoods and demolishing distressed public housing so you can reconstruct it in mixed income communities and establishing positive incentives for resident self-sufficiency and acquiring sites for off-site construction. Should I go on?"

"Well, I, yeah, why not?"

"Creating supportive service programs for those relocated as a result of revitalization or privatization—and that's enough. I close the book. All I can say is if you think a ranch house as old as yours is gonna escape demolition for purposes of revitalization by these idealistic young public and private entrepreneurs who are now devoting their lives to altering neighborhoods by re-development and by relocating their elders and other kinds of progress in this brave new world of upscaling enterprise, give yourself another thought, old buddy."

"I've got another thought," Nick said.

"What's that?"

"Do nothing once Cassie's safe. Tough it out."

"I don't honestly see how you can do nothing under the circumstances."

"Didn't somebody important once say that to do nothing is actually to do something when that's the right thing to do? Assuming of course that we catch up with this idealistic young operator and escape the complications his wife evidently initiated."

"Don't worry," Jackson said. "We'll catch up with him. I swear I sniffed the faint smell of him just beyond the desk of that elegant lady receptionist back there. I have a suspicion she was ready to give him away at one point, then had second thoughts."

The Foggy Bottom Brew Pub was not crowded. Jackson figured it was still a bit early for the dinner crowd, so at that point it must be serving mostly those civil servants from the various government departments near the square who were stopping in for a quick drink on their way home to rejuvenated Georgetown and other upscale Northwest neighborhoods. He took Nick's arm again and guided him to a table some distance from the door to avoid the chill that had followed them in. They both ordered a draft Samuel Adams. Nick suddenly leaned forward as though to stand up.

"What's the matter, buddy?" Jackson said.

"You're not going to believe this. That HUD guard must be clairvoyant for recommending this place. Unless somebody from upstairs phoned down to tell him who we're looking for and what to do about it discreetly."

"How's that?"

Nick sat back again. "Take your time to look, but I think our young friend is sitting over there at the table near the cash register, side view, I guess with two of his older HUD buddies or who knows. Only he seems to be growing a beard."

"You mean our friend Parker?"

"Unless I'm somehow mistaken, that's our man. Very much alive and apparently serving the cause of housing re-development in the nation's capital rather than Princeton, New Jersey. No great surprise. I suppose more satisfying professionally than working for your old man. Maybe more in tune with upscale progress as well. So what do we do now?"

"Well first we'd better make sure he's who he's supposed to be," Jackson said. "If it's really our man, all we actually need to know is the fact that he's alive, isn't that right? On the other hand, not to confront him for the sin of deception would be to deny ourselves a unique pleasure. I speak from my experience tracking down certain heads of state—you know the story."

"Only this guy's not the deceiver. His wife is."

"No, his wife's the false accuser. He's the deceiver in that he seems to have been deceiving his wife and others by pretending to be dead."

"Well, whatever he is, I'm perfectly willing to confront him for calling me and my neighbors in Queenston Park emotional rather than rational, typical Princeton people against change, ready to sacrifice our chance to raise real estate values and make much money and I don't remember what else. While his idea of change is bringing in one huge McMansion after another to hover over smaller neighbors happy with what they've had for years. But we can't go into all that here."

"Anyway, a challenge at our age is fun only if you do it with a light heart and much improvisation. Another thing I learned from experience. So just follow me."

Jackson stood up, counted out cash to lay on the bill, stepped aside to wait for Nick to join him, then crossed to the table near the cash register a half step ahead of him. When he came to a stop beside the table, the three men sitting there looked up in unison as though a trained chorus. Jackson pulled out his wallet. He flashed a card in one of its windows, then put it away.

"Ripaldo of Homeland Security," he said. "I believe one of you is Timothy Parker."

"That's me," Tim said. "What's it to you?"

"We've been looking for you," Jackson said. "I'm helping my friend here prepare a case against you for perpetrating a deception and bearing false witness."

"Huh?" Tim said. "What are you talking about?"

"I'm talking about the trouble you've brought into the lives of several worthy people recently, beginning with Nick Mandeville here, classical scholar residing peacefully with his wife in Princeton, New

Jersey, until you came along with grand ideas about building a huge McMansion next door to their modest home as you have next to other space-loving neighbors."

"Do I know you?" Tim said to Nick. "I don't think I do. Anyway, what's this character saying?"

"Of course you know me," Nick said. "You've drunk whiskey in my home. And I'm one of those hated people in Princeton you wrote about who are against change. Meaning the rampant progress of urban re-development in the so-called Athens of America."

"Well, now that you mention it, I remember drinking your whiskey and meeting you and your wife, but so what? Is this some kind of game you're playing? If it is, I'm not amused."

"No game," Jackson said. "Not since your wife accused my friend's wife of getting rid of you. That meant serious trouble."

Both of Tim's companions were smiling now. They clearly took it to be a joke.

"What my wife's done or not done is of no concern to me at this point," Tim said. "Our relation is in suspension, to put it mildly. We're not communicating."

"Well you'd better start communicating at least long enough to tell her you're alive," Jackson said. "I mean if you really are. Otherwise you may be subject to a conspiracy charge."

Tim wasn't smiling. "Conspiracy to do what?"

"Conspiracy by way of a false charge of homicide intended to intim-idate my friend here and his wife and prevent them from living out their days in peace and quiet under open skies rather than under the shadow of a huge neighboring McMansion that will challenge their share of the sun and the free access of those creatures of nature meant to enjoy their natural habitat. Isn't that right, Nicolas?"

"Their natural habitat in my backyard, that's right. Birds and beasts, companions to man since time immemorial when man is hospitable, but soon no longer as free as they once were in my Queenston Park neighborhood."

"Man can be a problem," Jackson said.

"And so can nature," Nick said. "Runoff water from rain and the creation of impervious ground by development can guide nature to flood the land more regularly by way of overflow from our brook that has been meandering since the Ice Age but is now the cause of new erosion and swampland in the backyards of myself and some of my neighbors."

Tim's companions had also given up smiling. "You two guys ought to go into politics," one of them said. "You're terrific demagogues."

"Is that right?" Jackson said. "Did you hear that, Mandeville? Now that we've established that Mr. Parker is apparently alive, I think we'd better get out of here before I find myself forced to call up headquarters and report these operators for disparaging politics. And here in the nation's capital. It may be a cliché, but I've always said get your heart in America or get your ass out."

"I'm ready to take off," Nick said. "I think our mission is over. It just makes me very uncomfortable to hear unpatriotic talk like that in these perilous times. What else have we got to protect us these days against the demagogues down here but our own demagoguery?"

"That's it," Jackson said. "In Demagoguery We Trust. Let me just say a final word to your young friend here. He'd better get his ass back to Princeton and call off his wife or, as the politicians say, there will be consequences. Do you get my message?"

Jackson didn't wait for an answer. He took Nick's arm and led him to the door. As they stepped out, somebody behind them yelled "Fuck you, asshole. Both of you."

Cassie hadn't been down to the brook at the lower edge of their lot since the previous spring when a week-long rainfall had caused the brook to rise above its banks and spread into the second channel it had cut across the lawn in recent years, creating a small island that was now flooded with swift brown water. She had come down to the rim of that flow and watched it rush through the fallen branches and flattened scrub on the island as it made its way through trees thick with age. The overflow had brought in all kinds of minor trash, the usual plastic bottles and containers, blue newspaper bags, bits of cardboard, but also an outdoor table backed up to embrace a tree, and an outdoor chair hooked to it with its bottom ripped open. Some tree trunks had a fringe of grasses, curled in at the base by the brook's invasion, but not one of the younger trees down there was leaning precariously. That's something, Cassie had said to herself, at least for the time being.

Now, in late fall, the branches were bare, the lawn pockmarked with brown patches where it had been cleared of leaves, the brook for the moment diminished, calm, almost motionless. The landscape seemed to belong to a poorer country, a wilder country that reminded her of the village plot her mother had brought to her father as part of her dowry. That didn't prove of any value in the Kavalla tobacco industry, too small, too off by itself, no water nearby, but it had pines and their aromas, and her father would sometimes take her along after school to sit beside him at the high end of the plot while he smoked one, maybe two cigarettes, and tried to explain to her why it was still important to be wary of kings and the extreme members of anybody's conservative party. Or he would sit there silently, past smoking, sometimes lying back with his hands behind his head, eyes closed, just smelling the pines, tired of history that day.

Then there were a few times when he'd actually talk about the trees, explaining that it had taken more than a decade after the war and the

civil war to make up for some of what those years had cost in lost for-
ests, burned for fuel or retaliation or finally for expanded housing, and
except for olive trees farther south and some grand plane trees, most
older trees had disappeared. The curious thing, he'd say, was that the tall
trees you might come across, at least where people actually lived, were
often protected as though shrines, and the forestry service, when vigilant
beyond bribery, could make life miserable for ambitious entrepreneurs.
Yet the forest fires burned on, year in and year out, and houses would
spring up suddenly where the land, really belonging to no one, was still
charred and waiting for reforestation. He'd sigh. Land was our common
treasure, our shared legacy. And trees were living things. How could you
deliberately set a tree on fire anymore than you could a man?

Would people in this town make fun of that thought? Cassie wondered. Call it sentimental? Anti-humanist? She also wondered what her
father, for his part, would make of Queenston Park with its broad lawns
and its tall trees, so many surviving yet so many on their way out. She
was pretty sure he'd think it a kind of green Eden still, a thing to be
grateful for, God's gift of life in various forms so the wise man could
learn what he had and where he belonged—at least for a while. Was that
close to what Nick also thought? They'd never really talked about trees,
only the brook every now and then depending on its mood, and the
sorry state of the lawn at that end of the lot. And of course the house,
his sometimes-plaything, his sometimes-retreat. But trees and land as a
legacy? She did remember standing with him on the patio one time to
gaze down toward the brook, hearing him quote from something he'd
just been reading that had moved him—was it in Faulkner?—about an
Indian chief who had inherited land passed down from the generations
before him but who was wise enough to know that nobody really owned
land that was in his care, even if he was steward of it for a lifetime, especially since he could at any moment pass it on to somebody else in ex-

change for a horse. Why had that thought saddened Nick so? Things lost at the end of a lifetime if not before? Anyway, the Indian chief seemed to believe in a lifetime of care.

She wished Nick would come home now that he didn't really have anymore business in Washington. When he called he'd sounded relieved, on a high, very pleased that he and his friend Ripaldo had been clever enough to track down their—what had he called him?—their quarry. And then the added pleasure of telephoning detective Masseli to tell him where things stood, which he said meant that she was now free to go out and give herself a night on the town with Amy or anybody else she chose for a celebratory drink and dinner. So when would he be coming home? Soon, he'd said, couldn't be sure at that point because he felt he owed Ripaldo and his wife an evening out, and that might have to be the next day, anyway he'd call again as soon as that obligation was settled and he knew what train he'd be taking—the voice affectionate, almost his usual voice, just a bit quick.

And then Detective Masseli showing up at the front door, very polite, low-voiced, hands crossed casually in front of him, just wanted to stop by with a bit of good news for her that he expected she already heard from her husband and to offer his thanks for her cooperation in a complicated case. No further comment on the past, no good wishes for the future, just a final assurance that she could be certain there was no longer a problem, no longer an issue, she was free to go anywhere she wanted to go. Right, no problem. Never mind Solar Estates preparing to rip up the house next door and erect God knows what under peculiar regulations, but what about the woman who'd falsely accused her, if that's what she'd actually done? Well, he advised against making too much of that. It was part of the complication, the lady wasn't exactly alone in what she'd reported, and there were certain personal issues involved—anyway, the criminal issue, so to speak, was over, and it wouldn't really be to her advantage to get into some kind of civil case if that's what she had in mind. Just his frank advice, OK? At least she hadn't said No Problem to that, even if a possible civil case hadn't crossed her mind. And at least he hadn't ended up saying he'd just been doing his job all along, even if that was true, though she suspected he'd had the good sense not to pursue her very closely once he began to study the family side of the family business called Solar Estates.

Since Amy was busy that evening, there'd be no night out on the town in her company. Anyway, she'd already had that bit of freedom without Nick's blessing, and it had ended up making things with Amy rather awkward, as, she decided, shared embarrassment had a way of doing. Of course it wasn't Amy's fault that the mathematical genius in Cottage Club had behaved the way he had, but Amy had apologized profusely nevertheless, especially for not having heard Cassie getting her coat in the hallway and heading for the front door, abrupt as it was. Her mind had been elsewhere at that moment, she'd said, deep into local politics, or at one point, to her surprise, into club politics. Dwight had told her in confidence about problems he was having with what he himself called his den of snobbish bonding. The press was now after Cottage Club for some reason. Before the two of them got around to working on the petitions they had in front of them, Dwight read her a clipping that picked out the club as one of the few that still required necessary affiliations and legacies in their selection process, and more damning, at least from one point of view, another clipping that described the club's annual lingerie party when members in various states of undress went cavorting for attention, what the clipping called good-looking boys wearing gift boxes over their genitals and salad-eating girls in black negligees. Chill, man, chill, the paper quoted somebody saying. Amy had laughed at that. Cassie hadn't. Dwight's problem, Amy said, was that the press reports were true, so as the club president on duty, how could Dwight challenge them? But he had to do something. He admitted in the end that saving his club, and confronting the legal issues threatening The Street more generally, now took precedence over the environmental work he had committed himself to. Amy had sighed over the phone. "At least his club was almost empty for the holiday break when we got there. Even if almost wasn't quite good enough in your case."

Their talk, amiable to the end, hadn't really moved on anywhere after that. The only time Cassie'd spoken to her since was when she called from her cell phone that morning to say, alas, she was busy that evening, but had a quick question: driving by Cassie's house on the way uptown, she'd noticed the Solar Estates sign back in a new place that had been cleared on the front lawn of the doomed house next door to Cassie's—did it mean what she thought? Cassie said she couldn't be sure, but that certainly made it look like the re-development of Queenston Park by that father and son team was back in business. Amy moaned, then said, "Do take care, dear," and hung up.

Nick was well beyond the Washington Cathedral and close to Wilson High, his original destination, when he decided it was time to turn around from this once-familiar territory, its adventures and its discontents, put that bit of nostalgia behind him once and for all and head back to his Georgetown hotel for cocktail hour. Crossing Macomb Street a second time made him slow down to catch his breath and finally stop halfway into the next block on Wisconsin Avenue. Victoria Halliday, 3817 Macomb Street, Vicky to the world of those lean high school days, so sharp, so wise for her age, so almost available. On the face of it, the idea of looking her up on Macomb Street made little sense because he had no idea whether she was actually living at her parents' address, though this had been the word at that fortieth reunion when he learned that she had married the graduate student at Georgetown, the older boy who had hovered behind her last days as his pinned companion and the cause of her returning the pin. Married him, divorced him, never remarried, ended up back in her parents' home to take care of them in their last days. He had kept up with her in a distant way through the years by news he picked up from high school fraternity brothers who stayed on in DC to make their modest fortunes as civil servants of one kind or another, and at the reunion a sorority sister of Vicky's had brought out a specific bit of news that he carried with him since as a kind of memento to the reality of that lost past: Vicky had told her over the phone that she wasn't planning to show up for the great event, but she'd thought about it, and yes, "her Nick" was one of those she'd miss seeing.

Hearing that Vicky had put it like that had made him suddenly look away from her gray-haired friend, then smile to himself before looking back—after all, maybe Vicky had just lost his last name for the moment. Anyway, that rush of memory hadn't kept him from feeling that tracking down Vicky would lead him to a dead end, both of them so far removed from where they once were that a meeting could only be awkward, maybe costly for what little nostalgia was left.

So why was he turning around now for a quick detour down Macomb Street? Sure, he'd been surprised by the surge of anticipation, the sudden sweet apparitions, that had come to him with the train's approach to the city earlier that week, but he still thought of the old neighborhood as rooted in his growing days only, left behind to blossom as it chose, another life sometimes sharply there in recollection but another life. And even back then his hope had focused on his going somewhere else when the moment was right. He may have had very little idea about where he might actually end up, but the vision of possibilities always showed him entering some college farther north and some world grander than what was offered by his Northwest Washington neighborhood of less opulent times, where most of his friends were planning to go into some form of local employment right after high school, good for a certain mild security in the same section of the city the rest of their lives.

The fact was, that undefined vision of something larger farther away had come to him late during those casual days in DC, and Vicky had been a certain catalyst for it, the only one he ever talked to about things beyond high school fraternity and sorority gossip: who was dating whom that week, who was being clever or weird or impossible, who was scoring points on the football field or the dance floor. Vicky actually talked about books, even novels, even the artists who had most influenced the portfolio of water colors she kept in secret—secret until the day they'd decided to go more or less steady and she'd brought it out to show him as a token of her partial commitment to their special relationship.

That was Vicky. She didn't call it partial, just didn't give herself completely, tender but protective in their intimate moments, refusing to settle for the expected, the ordinary prerogatives for those supposedly going steady, because she couldn't yet be sure it would last very long, it never seemed to, and she wasn't ready to promise more than she believed was possible or grant more than she honestly felt she should. When he finally found the courage to talk to her about where their feelings for each other might lead, she'd said she didn't know, just too hard to answer a question like that—and this was well before her graduate school admirer appeared on the scene to complicate the question further in obvious ways. She said the truth was, they'd be graduating soon, and he'd be going off to some new life elsewhere, an open life free of the prejudices around them and with the horizons broader, surely what he ought to do, and then that would have to be the end between them because she had to find her own place to go for more learning, nearer home, less expensive and less demanding than what he had in mind. He could now call her a realist with an aversion to pretense and a heart full of good sense, but it confused him at the time, failed to fulfill the romantic image of his hope, and if it taught him in the end to be as wary as she was of pretenders and deceivers and to honor truth with the right passion, it had left him empty when he finally moved away. A special relationship, no question about it while it lasted, but he chose Princeton over Georgetown, as she knew he would. Now, after all this time, he could use a shot of her insight about pretenders and a dash of her good sense—that is, if he could still find her.

Her house, her parents' house, was unchanged, at least from the front: the left half of a duplex, the front door at the top of steps rising beside the basement to the first of two brick stories well above street level. The windows were blank up front on both floors, but there was a hint of indoor light beyond the ground floor living room, where the kitchen used to be. If Vicky was there, she must be resting, or maybe reading in one of the back rooms upstairs by what outside light was left that afternoon. He climbed the front steps and pressed the bell, waited a decent time, then pressed it again. He heard somebody coming down the stairs from the second floor. The door opened sharply. A middle-aged woman in what seemed a partial nurse's uniform stood there gazing at him.

"Yes?" she said.

"I'm looking for Victoria Halliday. She used to live here. I don't know her married name."

"Mrs. Victoria Constable lives here. What's your business? You don't sound like a relative."

"Just a friend. I'd like to have a word with her. Is that possible?"

"Well, that may be and that may not be. She's not well."

"I don't want to disturb her. I just…"

"What's your name?"

"Nick. Nicholas Mandeville."

The woman was studying him. "Well, sir. You wait here and I'll see what I can do. Which may not be much since you're not a relative."

She left the front door ajar. When she appeared again at the foot of the stairs, she signaled him to follow her. At the top of the stairs, she pointed toward the front room, then stepped around him and disappeared. Vicky was sitting up in bed, a hospital bed with the back raised, it seemed, as far up as it could go. There was a book on the bed. Her legs were under the covers, her robe tight around her, but one arm, crossed over the other, was partially exposed: thin, spotted, the hand curled almost like a claw. Her gray hair was cropped, her face drawn, the cheekbones sharp, but he could still see an approximation of the face he knew. She was smiling broadly.

"Nicholas, I knew it had to be you, I just couldn't quite believe it. I'm truly surprised. I didn't want you to see me like this, but I wasn't going to miss the chance of it being you."

"Well. Vicky. I don't know what to say. I was just passing through and I ..."

"Never mind. You don't have to explain. You're somehow here, and I guess that says enough."

Nick looked around for a chair. There was no chair.

"Sit at the foot of the bed," Vicky said. "I'm not contagious. It's just cancer."

"Just cancer? How can you say a thing like that? I mean, I..."

"I guess I'm getting used to it. Not that I really like talking about it. How did you know I was living where I used to live, I mean where my parents used to live?"

"I didn't know. I just, well I just took a chance on finding you when I crossed Macomb. On the way back to my hotel. Anyway."

She shifted the pillow so her back was a touch straighter. "OK. So now you can tell me why you're really here. Nicholas Vaudeville. Mandeville. Whatever. Once my Nick. God, that was a long time ago."

"Yes. And it was all over rather abruptly. Too abruptly."

"Well, you left town and went north to make your fortune, right? What did you expect?"

"Some fortune. I'm still working on that, in a manner of speaking. I'm thinking of retiring early to have time for writing a book. My travels in Never-Neverland. Something like that. I won't bore you with the details."

"Don't. Write it. Just write it. Don't waste what may be there talking about it. Not to me or anybody."

"There are a few problems I have to cope with first. Like protecting my house from the megabuilders who are taking over my neighborhood. And not only my neighborhood. A good slice of the country."

"Is that right? That's one thing I don't have to worry about. This is the house where I was born and the house where I'm going to die. And no time left for worrying about where to live or where to travel. Which may be a blessing."

"You don't really mean that. You…"

"Yes I do. You'll see. Staying where you are and not being able to go anywhere concentrates the mind, as they say. At some point I think you'll come to see that the mega this or that won't make much difference any longer. You'll find the mega peace."

"Tell me about that."

"Well, I suppose it's what some people still call the peace that passes understanding, but I find that a bit corny. A hangover from the time I knew you, when we used to go to church once in a while. Now I don't know what to call it. I just know what it is. But it's really too personal to talk about."

"I wish you would. It might help me."

Vicky half smiled. "You don't look as though you need help. You look fine. Anyway, compared to the way I look."

Nick reached to take her hand. It felt cold, but it could still hold on, for a second.

"I don't know," she said. "It's just that you finally shift from thinking about where you could go or even should go and think about where you've been and how much it's meant to you, some of it anyway. Call it a shift toward being sort of grateful for what you've had. But I can't explain it. You'll just have to wait until it comes to you. That is, if you're lucky enough before it's too late."

Cassie suddenly felt discouraged by her survey of the backyard. Just the size of the cleared area intimidated her if she was actually to plant a border on both sides of it, the one side extending beyond the pachysandra toward the low ground by the brook, the other a safer distance from the brook but not as open to sunlight. The problem on all sides of that lawn was what would best thrive there beside the smattering of crocuses and daffodils and the string of azaleas left over from the original owner, the retired army colonel who'd scattered his—or his wife's—bulbs rather casually while apparently focusing on the corner of the yard nearest the house to serve a pleasure of his as he got older. That was where there had once been a small circle of lawn with a cement-lined hole in the center, the grass in the circle tight as a carpet when they'd first moved in. Nick had said it was obviously kept that way for the retired owner to practice his golf, and he'd been amused by the eccentricity of a luxury like that in the backyard of a ranch house on the less pretentious side of Princeton. Nick had played around out there for a while with some clubs his father had left him, but that circle had disappeared long ago, overgrown and eventually returned to nature from lack of special attention by the Italian gardener who took care of the lawn, which didn't really make her feel guilty for a second.

To go ahead, she would simply have to do more research, learn what others recommended for the kind of clay soil in their neighborhood, what plantings could best survive the droughts and heavy rains and stormwater runoff on impermeable surfaces, as they'd called the problem at that township environmental meeting. Also what plantings could live through a summer and longer if she and Nick took up traveling again as Nick had suggested they might want to do at some point. As far as she was concerned, there were things to settle before they could really think about traveling anywhere. Beginning with the—how to put it?— the resurrection of Randy Parker and his Solar Estates.

God knows she'd tried to put him off when he called, maybe not hard enough from the start, the excuse of Nick's not being back home yet from Washington failing too easily when the man insisted she was the one he wanted to talk to however briefly, she was the one he owed an apology for what had been a failure of communication that really had nothing to do with her, a complete misunderstanding that he hoped she would give him a chance to explain to their mutual benefit. What could she do? Refuse to see him on the same grounds that she really had to consult her husband first? Throw his attempt to apologize back in his face when it might be the wrong face? What was there to lose by treating him decently as a human being whatever she thought of him? The answer in the end had to be who she herself should try to be and how she should show herself.

So she wasn't going to worry about having agreed to see him— though not inside the house while she was alone, she hadn't gone that far, just out back on the garden patio or beyond where she'd told him she was planning to spend the late afternoon doing some informal surveying of the land back there, the trees along the property line and who they belonged to, what living trees remained along the brook, how the gathering problem of debris from overflow was progressing, etc., that's where he'd find her. If he showed up. It was getting cool now and darker. She wasn't about to wait much longer however much he—speak of the devil.

"Sorry I'm a bit late," Randy Parker said. "I got involved checking on a few last-minute things next door."

He extended his hand. She took it, limply.

"So you're going to start building next door any minute, is that it?"

"Not me. My son Tim. It's strictly his project from now on. Which is what I wanted to talk to you about. Can I sit down?"

"Of course. The chairs aren't as clean as they ought to be out here, but help yourself. I prefer to stand. For exercise."

Randy unfolded a chair. He looked at the seat, brushed it vaguely with his hand, sat down, leaned forward.

"The point is, as I think I began to explain over the phone, it was all a family squabble that got out of hand. You know what I mean?"

"Well, I know what family squabbles are but I don't know what you're talking about."

"What I'm talking about is the argument between my son and daughter-in-law that led to his temporary departure from our family business and his wife's temporary nuttiness, if I can use that word for it. Anyway, I won't go into the details because he's back in our business now and they're back together, for which I have to thank your husband at least in part."

"My husband?"

"Well, he was the one who traced the boy back to his old government hangout in Washington, DC, and must have done something to wise the lad up. Anyway, Tim's back home now and back at work for the family business and I owe your husband one for that. In fact, the boy now seems so settled in up here that he and his lady are thinking in the end they might keep the house they're going to build next door to you. I mean keep it for themselves."

"Wouldn't that be lovely," Cassie said. "The couple that wrongly accuses you moves in next door and we all end up a happy family."

"Well, the thing is, it wasn't the couple really, it was Sheila, and she didn't really accuse anyone of anything. She just lost her cool when Tim walked out on her after she complained to him about some of his public statements and his difficulties with the community here—I won't mention any names—she ended up getting defensive so that after he disappeared completely she told some stuff to the police she probably shouldn't have because the truth is, she didn't know what to do. I mean she lost her head. Not that I'm here to defend the way she behaved in the end."

"So why are you here, Mr. Parker?"

"Well, first of all I want to apologize to you in person for the trouble this business may have caused you and then I want to make you a serious new offer for your place. Not in compensation, mind you, but simply in gratitude and hopefully to bring this whole thing to a kind of closure."

"The only closure that interests me is an end to what McMansion development is doing to our neighborhood."

Randy sat back in his chair. "I understand how you and a few others around here feel but I'm afraid you're all living in dream land. I promise you, if it isn't Solar Estates working to revitalize the neighborhood, it will be somebody else moving in for their own kind of upgrading. The lots in your neighborhood are just too valuable, and—forgive me—the houses are too old and small. Someday soon they will have to come down, and I'm afraid that includes yours."

"Not as long as I can prevent it," Cassie said.

"Dear lady, my point is that you can't prevent it. Whether you like it or not, things in this country move forward. People want to realize their assets in the free market way. And the old will always have to yield to the new in the end, so the sooner the better if there's going to be progress. My role in life is to help that happen."

"As far as I'm concerned, your role in life is to make money."

"You can put it that way if you want, but selling your house to Tim and me would certainly be for your financial benefit as well as ours. More yours than ours, considering what we have to invest in time and cost."

"My God, how can that be? By selling you this house for $700,000 so that you can build one for $2,500,000 in its place, as you've advertised that monstrous house on Independence Road? And whatever we get for this house we would have to spend on a new one, if not more?"

"Well, if you're willing to listen to reason, dear lady, that $700,000 could become $800,000 tomorrow and no strings attached. That's my offer. Even though the housing market happens to be going down at the moment. And considering that you probably paid no more than $50,000 for this house in the first place however many years ago, check the mathematics."

"But what you don't seem to understand is that I don't want the money, I want the house. Our house. As it is."

"Sure," Randy said, smiling stiffly. "For how long as it is? I'm sorry to say it, but the place is already falling apart. I could tell that from the quick look inside you allowed me and Tim. The cracks here and there, the cork floor, the heating problem..."

"It has lasted this long, it will last a while longer. At least as long as I last."

Randy stood up. He was no longer smiling.

"Well, if I can't tempt you, maybe I can tempt your husband. For the good of all of us, including your beautiful Queenston Park. When do you expect him back?"

"None of your business, really. You just don't give up, do you?"

Randy sighed, shook his head, stood up and raised his hand in a quick salute, said "God bless," then crossed in front of her to disappear beyond the thick trunk of the tree at the far edge of the patio.

Nick decided he'd seen enough: half the house was gone, most of the roof was gone on the near side, the garage was still standing but surely next in line for demolition as soon as the rest of the house vanished, the sounds of that final violent teardown no doubt rising grandly just beyond the footprint of the new garage drafted to go up closer to the border of his own house, as permitted by current regulations. He turned back and headed in the opposite direction, reversing his usual path when his daily walk was delayed until after dark. The moon was up, there was light enough in either direction, but he planned to make this a short one, just a few blocks along that side of Queenston Park down to the bridge across Harry's Brook. The dinner at Lahiere's with Cassie had been better than good for both of them, Nick thought—duck, rack of lamb, standard stuff but done right—and the wine the waiter had recommended was more than palatable, anyway right for the easy-going intimacy he'd hoped for on his first night back home. Not that he'd been gone that long, but he couldn't be certain that Cassie would prove as reasonable about it all as she did prove, apparently so unconcerned about his having taken his time getting back that he'd actually stopped feeling the small pang of guilt that had cut into his return train ride to keep him a bit on edge even after he'd spotted her waiting on the far side of the Dinky tracks.

What had occupied his thinking during the train ride home was just how much of his intimate reunion with Vicky he felt he should share with Cassie, if anything at all. Talking about Vicky's warm reception and what she had said during that deathbed meeting—her confident sense of place, the peace she had finally discovered—he would surely show how much it had moved him. And to make the reasons for his response clear to his wife, the history that colored the occasion and its ultimate innocence might be more than he could handle as delicately as he would like. He decided that it might be better just to leave that episode out of his account of the time he'd spent touring his old haunts and reminiscing with Ripaldo. It was enough that his meeting with Vicky had caused him to focus more on being grateful for what he had and less on where he might want to go, as she'd put it. What he had that was best of all he knew again the minute he saw her: his Cassie, and her particular wisdom.

He hadn't been sure at first that she'd spotted him across the Dinky tracks because she'd just stood there stone still, no expression he could make out, as though she didn't recognize him, and then he remembered that he was wearing the hat and scarf he'd bought in Georgetown when the weather down there suddenly turned chilly, which must have disguised him until he took the hat off and waved. She'd still waited until he reached her side of the tracks before she took a step and moved into him silently, wrapping her arms around him as tight as he could want, then handed him her car key. And the account of her days while he was gone, weaving in and out of his own account, was warm, mostly lively, anyway uncomplaining, so that the ride in from Princeton Junction to Queenston Park and their first hour together had settled him down completely.

He was amused that she'd been bold enough, as she put it, to go uptown with Amy to visit Cottage Club while it was more or less empty and that she'd found it rather old-fashioned in its décor, rather British. So much for F. Scott Fitzgerald's Jazz Age aura. And Amy had apparently

proven to be a good companion for some discreet shopping here and
there until she became preoccupied, according to Cassie, with preparing
to run for the Township Committee in keeping with what her environmental group had decided was the only way to try to accomplish something serious in the Township of Princeton, given how democracy was
arranged in their portion of New Jersey. Well, may the gods be with us
in that. And with Detective Masseli after his assurance that Cassie had
nothing more to worry about as long as she didn't get herself involved
in any sort of civil case or appeal to the authorities because the situation
was complicated and she was bound to lose. He obviously knew what
he was talking about. Anyway, one complication surely no longer subject to appeal before man, nature, or whatever resided beyond, was the
pending arrival of a McMansion next door, now apparently approved
for construction by all relevant agencies in the township, along with the
destruction of the humble house over there already half done. It was,
simply put, a done deal.

But the business with Randy Parker still gnawed at him most of
all. He wasn't one bit happy about that operator having dropped in on
Cassie specifically while he was out of town, going after her to apologize
with a proposal up his sleeve, a hungry suitor for her favor with an offer
he seemed to think she couldn't refuse even before she'd consulted her
husband. Well, he'd met his match in Cassie, whether he accepted it or
not. And the audacity of following up on that private encounter with an
e-mail headed "Dear Professor," hoping the four of them—prodigal son
Tim presumably the fourth—could get together when convenient once
the professor was home, because there was serious business to discuss
now that his boy Tim was back in the family. And then with perfect tim-
ing, some snake in the grass working next door ruined their afternoon
siesta by bringing in the rasping sound of handsaws cutting away at
some huge tree in their former neighbor's front yard so that the hovering

bulldozer or backhoe or whatever monstrosity was out there could better thrust ahead through the remnant trees to strike the next violent blow against the house that was on its way to oblivion.

In some earlier phase of his life those sounds could have driven him to cross the border of reason and force whoever was in charge over there to listen to a harangue about the cost of what his boss was bringing forth against nature, make him try to see the full unrecorded expense of his boss's creation, but what good would that do now? Especially since it turned out that the boss of the moment wasn't Randy Parker but the apple of his eye, Tim, liberated from the revitalization and privatization of public housing and back in the fold to make his fortune in the free enterprise re-development and upgrading of Queenston Park. It was cutting irony that he himself had helped to free the prodigal son for his return to this more profitable career, not the best thing for one's morale on a moonlit night. And the thought of him and his wife moving in next door. Good God. Was it Auden who had insisted that the only essential Christian belief was in loving your neighbor as yourself? OK. But even when Solar Estates is your next door neighbor? Impervious builders Tim and Sheila Parker? Didn't that ask too much? Or was being asked too much and learning to live with it the whole point? He'd have to count on Cassie and her faith to help straighten that one out first chance they had to—

"You walk too fast," Cassie said behind him, short of breath. "I could barely catch up to you without running."

"Well, I didn't know you planned on joining me. Sweet surprise."

She took his arm. "I didn't know either. It was the ghosts next door that drove me out. I'm not kidding."

"The ghosts?"

"Voices I could swear were of the Truex couple that used to live there. The old man who worked his heart out on that beautiful garden that's doomed now, who kept it trim even after his wife died. And I could swear I saw a flickering light in the piece of the house that's still standing. That's when I stepped out on the patio and heard the voices over there."

"How do you know it wasn't our future neighbors checking the place out? Tim Parker and his wife, for example."

"Talking low like that? In what sounded like a foreign language? Under candlelight?"

"Well, there wouldn't be any electricity operating over there now. Besides—but what do I know? O. K, let's say it's those two old souls come back for a final look. Though I find it sad to believe that."

"You see, I knew you could believe it if you tried hard enough. It's really very spooky. I turned off all our lights. Not that it's about to scare me away. Nothing can do that. I'm staying put where I belong."

"Same here."

"Is that so? I thought you wanted us to go traveling around the world sometime soon."

"Not the whole world. Just the parts we used to know or still want to know. But right now I'm not planning to go anywhere."

She squeezed his arm. "I'm so glad to hear that. I don't want to go anywhere right now either. I don't want to let anybody think for a minute that they've won us over."

"I'm with you there. So we just stay put as long as we can. Except for a vacation every now and then. Treat ourselves to what good things there are while we still have time, as our ancient friend Semonides said God knows how many centuries ago."

"So can we go back home now? I don't want whoever's next door to think we're really afraid."

"Sure. We'll go back and turn on the lights. Show that we welcome neighbors whoever they may be. Since we're told you have to love your neighbors as you love yourself. So long as— "

"So long as they love trees and animals and gardens as much as they love themselves, OK?"

"OK."

He took her hand and turned back toward their house, guiding her slowly along the margin of the newly paved street on that side of Queenston Park.

Edmund Keeley

photo by Mary Cross

ABOUT THE Author

Edmund Keeley, who lives in Princeton, N.J., is the author of eight novels, fifteen volumes of poetry and fiction in translation, and ten volumes of non-fiction. Though his work often makes use of the culture and landscape of Greece, several novels are partially set in the U.S., and one focuses on Southeast Asia. His first work of historical non-fiction, *The Salonika Bay Murder*, is an account of the circumstances surrounding the murder of CBS correspondent George Polk during the Greek Civil War. A recent memoir, *Borderlines*, tells the story of his childhood as the son of a U.S. Foreign Service officer in Canada, Greece, and Washington, D.C., and his later education at Princeton and Oxford.

Keeley's first novel, *The Libation*, received the Rome Prize of the American Academy of Arts and Letters. His translations of contemporary Greek poets earned him the Harold Morton Landon Award of the Academy of American Poets, the First EEC Prize for the translation of Poetry, and the PEN Ralph Manheim Medal for Translation. In 1999 he was honored for "exceptional accomplishment" by the American Academy of Arts and Letters, and in 2001 the President of Greece named him a Commander of the Order of the Phoenix.

Keeley taught English and Creative Writing at Princeton from 1954 to 1994 and served for some years as Director of Creative Writing and Director of Hellenic Studies. He was twice President of the Modern Greek Studies Association and was President of PEN American Center from 1992-94. On eleven occasions he served as American delegate at International PEN congresses. During his retirement he continues to write regularly and to travel to new and old places.

CPSIA information can be obtained at www.ICGtesting.com
Printed in the USA
BVOW02s0444280314

349055BV00002B/35/P